First

Last

Forever

A Collection of First Date Disasters

The Space City Scribes:

Mandy Broughton

Artemis Greenleaf

Ellen Leventhal

K. C. Maguire

Ellen Rothberg

Monica Shaughnessy

PUBLISHED BY:
Black Mare Books
Houston, Texas
www.blackmarebooks.com

ISBN: 978-1-941502-79-2
First Last Forever
Copyright © 2016 by
Mandy Broughton, Artemis Greenleaf, Ellen Leventhal,
K.C. Maguire, Monica Shaughnessy

Contents

First

Last

Forever

First

First dates open the door to the promise of a new beginning.

Valentine's Date

K.C. Maguire

THE SANDWICHES at the receptionist's desk don't look too bad tonight, but I'm going to resist. They're supposed to be for attorneys who plan to work late, not for folks trying to sneak out at the incredibly early hour of 7:00pm. That's why they don't set them out until 6-ish. They're from the deli downstairs. I can see one of their signature cream cheese, dried apricot, and walnut on sourdough at the edge of the tray. Usually my downfall, but not tonight.

I promised myself I'd go out to this thing if only to get my sister to shut up about my sadly single status. If I don't put in an appearance at the young professional mingle and score at least one phone number, I'll never hear the end of it. I've told her I don't have time to date, but no dice. She's already on her third fiancé in eight years which has to be some kind of record, but at least she always has a date.

I heave my backpack over my shoulder and grunt under the weight. I've left my Uggs inside the bag in favor of wearing my kitten heel boots. The mingle is only two blocks away and I don't want to change shoes when I get there. My long wool coat should keep my legs warm enough. Avoiding the small crowd of pasty-faced older attorneys picking at the sandwiches, I slip into the shadows and follow the inside corridor to the elevator bank. The walls here gleam in polished mahogany with gold accents. No expense spared on the parts of the building the clients actually see. Of course my own office is closet sized and the ochre paint is peeling and bubbling. I only see clients in the art deco conference room. If I stick with it another year or so, I'm told I'll graduate to a walk-in-pantry sized office with a window. Once in the elevator, my toes beat an involuntary tattoo against the floor tiles.

I scan my reflection in the stainless steel elevator door. Unable to tame my wild mop of curly hair, I've drawn it up into a scrunchy. I'm going for a "classy, but I don't care" persona, at least that's what I tell myself.

Underneath my burgundy coat, I'm sporting the uniform of all sensible female lawyers: the basic black polyester skirt-suit that never creases or wrinkles, and never has to be ironed. It retains heat like nobody's business, but it looks respectable. I haven't bothered with makeup. I hardly ever do. My face is alright without it, I suppose. Occasionally, I swipe on a sheen of lip gloss, but that's only going to rub off on the first glass of booze. And I'm going to need alcohol to get through this thing. My eyes are my best feature, a mixed blue-green color with hazel tints around the irises. The only problem is they're hard to see through my glasses. I should get contacts, but I can't be bothered. Perhaps if I start dating, it'll give me the incentive I need.

I don't even want to think about the last time I went on a real date. I haven't dated seriously since I started at Fletcher, Fleischman & Co. I tell myself I don't have the time, but I know that's an excuse, at least that's how my sister sees it. I prefer to see myself as a harried professional moving up the corporate law ladder with limited time for a personal life.

When the elevator doors open, the first thing I do is slip on the lobby tiles. An embarrassed flush rises in my neck, but I straighten up and focus. The foyer is relatively empty, just the receptionist and a few stragglers dotted around the place. A Christmas tree still looms large in the alcove even though the holiday came and went a couple of weeks ago. Someone has finally removed the stack of fake presents from around its base. My backpack catches in the revolving door on the way out. Maybe it's an omen that I should have stayed in the office with my sandwiches, my refinancing project, and my timesheets.

Luckily, there's no snow in the forecast. It's been an unseasonably warm winter, although Cleveland can be unpredictable at the best of times. One of my boss's favorite sayings is: "If you don't like our weather, wait a minute." It always gets a forced chuckle out of his underlings, and clients.

A chill wind tugs my jacket, and I pull it tighter around myself as I bundle down the block toward the offices of Butler Kline and Roosevelt, who are hosting the mingle. They're charging money for attendance so it's a win-win for them regardless of whether anyone finds true love. They introduce folks to their recently renovated offices – prospective clients and maybe even a few lateral hires – as well as earning goodwill from the young professional community, and earning some pocket change in the process. I wonder how they got the Bar to sign off on a firm charging for a social event.

Before I know it, I'm crossing the threshold of the Butler Kline foyer. No Christmas trees here, just miles and miles of polished marble. Their lobby is dark green and silver in contrast to our more somber gray and black. A festively decorated sign points to a staircase beyond the elevator bank. The big do is on a Mezzanine level.

Like a prisoner mounting the gallows, I trudge up the staircase. At the top, I hear voices and the sound of glasses clinking. I follow more signs around a bend in the landing, and the space opens out before me. The mezzanine is a cut-away level with floor to ceiling windows and a plush carpet. My heels are already sinking into it. There must be 40 or 50 people here already. They're clustered into comfortable-looking groups, so I suspect some folks came with people they already knew. I was too embarrassed to tell anyone else I was coming. Most of my friends are already paired off, so I'm not expecting to see anyone I know, at least no one I know well.

Piles of jackets and bags line benches on the far wall so I head in that direction, unbuttoning my coat on the way. I'm stopped by a guy with curly hair in a pin-striped business suit and a cream satin tie loosened around his neck.

"Hi, I'm Marc Watkins. Can I get you a drink?" he says.

Wow, this guy's off to a quick start.

I'm about to respond when my backpack slips from my shoulder and jars my elbow.

"Here, let me help you," he says as he reaches for the strap. His movements are ungainly, perhaps because he's so tall. He reminds me a little of a grasshopper, all crooked angles: a pin-stripy insect.

"No, I've got it." I yank the strap away from him, causing him to spill his drink, some of which dribbles on my jacket.

"Oops. Let me take care of that." With an exaggerated flourish, he produces an old-fashioned handkerchief from his breast pocket and leans over to press it to my chest with a little too much enthusiasm.

I back away. "No, thanks. It would be better if I washed it."

His face falls for a moment before sparking to life again. "I'll show you to the restroom. What's your name?"

"Hannah," I say, wondering belatedly if I should have made something up. "Why don't you point me to the restroom? I'll catch you later, okay?"

"Promise?" It's only one word, but the way he says it, it sounds like he's requesting me to enter into an ironclad contract.

"Yeah, okay," I say, crossing my fingers inside my coat pocket.

"Over there. Women's on the left, men's on the right." He points to an alcove beyond the benches. Then squeezes my elbow in a way that's a little too familiar. "I'll be waiting."

You'll be waiting a while.

I hurry away in the direction he indicated. That was dark beer he spilled, and it's going to stain. If it does, I'm sending the dry-cleaning bill to my sister.

Elevator music pipes through the restrooms here. Classy. I try to make out the tune. It's either "The Girl from Ipanema" or some reggae version of "Material Girl." I wet a hand towel and blot at my coat. The stain fades but doesn't disappear completely. I curse under my breath. Absorbed in my task, I don't notice when the other girl comes in until she turns on the faucet beside me. We make eye contact in the mirror. She looks about my age, but better put-together: blonde streaked hair draped loose over her shoulders and a little subtle makeup, gloss and mascara. Same uniform as me, though: wrinkle free business attire.

"Hi?" she says, making it sound like a question.

"Umm. Hi." I return my focus to the stain.

"That looks pretty bad," she says, reaching for a towel to dry her hands. "You could try baking soda. My mom swears by it."

"Yeah?" I pretend to sound interested.

"How did you do it? You don't look like a dark beer girl," she says, collecting a clutch purse from the counter. Looks like something expensive, but it's probably a knock-off. Junior associate salaries aren't as high as people think.

"It was this guy," I say.

"Marc Watkins?"

"How did you guess?"

"He hits on all the newbies. And he's a walking disaster area."

"You can say that again." I grimace.

"But he's harmless," she says. "Just a bit over-eager, you know. I'm Lacey." She reaches out a hand for me to shake.

"Hannah."

"You are a newbie, right?" she asks.

I nod.

"So what's your excuse?"

This time, I raise a questioning eyebrow.

"Nagging mother." She points to herself in clarification.

Oh.

"Mom and sister," I say, pointing to myself in the same way.

"Want me to introduce you around?" she says.

"Actually, I was just -- "

"Thinking of leaving? I know. I felt like that at the first one of these I came to, but there are some nice folks here if you know who to talk to. You should have a drink and get your money's worth before you motor."

"Can we avoid that guy?" I ask.

"Safety in numbers, right? Don't worry. My friends and I will protect you."

"Okay, I guess."

Lacey's as good as her word. She introduces me to a group of young lawyers she refers to as "the regulars." Mostly women, but a couple of guys. A lot of them work at Lacey's firm: McCartney, Lyme & Co. Their offices are on the west side. They carpool to these things. They're going for dinner afterwards and invite me to join them. I tell them I'll think about it. After a few more drinks and a little more discussion, they decide to head out. And that means I'm losing my shield against Marc. If they're out of here, I'm losing my protection against him. I've noticed him glancing at me a couple of times, but Lacey or her friends always manage to block him when he tries to approach. It's either dinner with them or go home alone. Dinner's beginning to sound better and better.

We're collecting our coats and bags when my luck runs out. There's a tap on my shoulder, and Marc's right there.

"Hannah?" he asks. He smells of beer along with a faint scent of mint.

Lacey groans beside me and mouths "Sorry."

"You leaving already? I was hoping we could chat." He looks so crestfallen I almost feel bad for him.

"Maybe next time," I say, trying to copy the trick Lacey's friends have used and giving him my back. He blocks me with his shoulder so I'm stuck between him and the table.

"How about I give you my number, or my email?" he says. "I'd really like to talk."

I look to Lacey, and she's making a winding motion with her hands to give him the idea we need to hurry. He seems oblivious. Before I know it, Marc is pressing a business card into my jacket pocket.

He leans in to whisper in my ear, "My personal cellphone number is on the back."

He draws away and winks.

"Thanks," I say out of reflex.

"Call me," he says, doing the matching hand-gesture.

Is this guy for real? I'm almost tempted to look around for a hidden camera.

Lacey grabs my hand and steers me to the stairway.

"Seriously, what's wrong with him?" I ask her.

"He's okay. Really," she says. "Most of us have actually dated him once or twice."

"What?"

"Well, we've all been newbies at these things. Desperate and dateless and all that," she says. "And he's not a bad guy, in the right light and after a few glasses of alcohol."

"How many glasses does it take?" I ask.

She laughs.

"I don't think I'm quite that desperate yet," I say.

"Never say never." She grins, exposing a tiny gap between her front teeth. It reminds me of the Cheshire Cat.

"You guys coming or what?" One of her friends calls from the bottom of the stairs.

"Come on," Lacey says, dragging me down the stairs. "Sustenance awaits."

I can't believe how quickly work picks up after the holidays. It's as if everyone was saving up their legal issues for the New Year. Piles of documents filter down through the partners' offices and end up on my desk. Since the mingle, my days have at least been punctuated by light-hearted bantering emails from Lacey, particularly her ongoing series of digital tirades about not having a date for Valentine's Day which is less than three weeks away now. Her latest missive is open on my screen as I scan through a set of re-financing documents.

Too, too single? Need to mingle? Come to the meet and greet on Valentine's Day! At least you can say you're ~~married~~ *– DESPERATE!!!*

It's hard to believe that the organizers actually set up an event for Valentine's Day in a last ditch effort to match up all the single lawyers in town at the eleventh hour. Lacey thinks we should go as a joke, or at least to present a united front.

I scan the other new message in my inbox. From Marc. Yes, that Marc. I've been bantering with him too since the mingle. He tracked down my email address from the participant list. I have to admit he's not a bad email correspondent as long as we stick to simply being virtual pen-pals. He has an okay sense of humor, and most of his messages are professional and friendly. Our running joke is about making a computer game out of our experiences on the partnership track. We're torn between a "Sonic the Hedgehog"-style platform game and a good old-fashioned shoot 'em up.

His message reads:

C'mon, Kiddo. I know you're busy, but you've got to eat. And you can't be planning to work all night on Valentine's Day. Let me cook for you. Dinner will be on the table whether you come or not, and I hate to eat alone.

Lacey says Marc's problem is that he gets nervous in crowds. He's much better one-on-one and I'm beginning to maybe believe her. Maybe. She says that even if he's not "Mr. Right," maybe he could be "Mr. Right-Now." It's hard to know whether she's joking. I can never get her to be serious about this stuff.

Dropping my red pen onto on my desk, I let my fingers hover over the keyboard for a second before calling up Lacey's email to respond.

Can't do the Valentine's mingle with you. The man-of-my-dreams invited me for dinner.
☺

Her reply pings onscreen in moments.

You mean Marc??? What's he got that I don't?
And it's on …

ME: *You really want me to spell it out?*
LACEY: *In graphic detail.*
ME: *Thought you'd already seen it?*
LACEY: *A lady never tells.*

Before I can respond, she sends a follow-up message.

LACEY: *But seriously, are you going to give him a chance?*

I stop to think. We've only been kidding around, haven't we? I wasn't seriously going to accept his invitation. I tap the nib of my pen on my desktop. What should I say now? I'm not really going to have a Valentine's date with Marc, am I? No, I'd rather stay desperate and dateless this year.

No, Honeybunch, I've decided. Valentine's mingle it is for us, I type back to Lacey.

I stare at the screen but she doesn't respond.

I wait … and wait … and wait.

And then I take a closer look at my screen. My eyes widen. Lacey's message is still there, open in a textbox. Marc's message has disappeared.

Holy cannoli! I didn't. I couldn't have.

I move the cursor to my sent folder, but an incoming message pops up before I have a chance to open it. It's from Marc.

Delighted to hear it, Honeybunch. Can't wait to cook for you.

Crap, crap, crap, crap, crap. I'm not that much of a space cadet, am I?

I didn't! I couldn't have!

I did.

Marc is replying to the message I thought I'd sent to Lacey. He thinks I want to mingle with him on Valentine's Day … and that I called him "Honeybunch."

My heart sinks.

What am I supposed to do now? I can't very well tell him I accepted his invitation thinking I was writing to Lacey.

I forward the whole message chain to her to show her what happened, and to ask her advice.

Her answer is simple.

You made your bed, HONEYBUNCH. Now you have to lie in it.

☺

Marc instructed me to arrive at 7:30 and dress casual. I'm early because I'm so eager to get this over with. Lacey kept reiterating that Marc's harmless and if I have a few glasses of wine and let myself relax, I might surprise myself and have fun. She's not going to the mingle after all. She and her other friends are going out for "sad and sorrowful" drinks. She said to join them later if my date is a bust.

He lives in a neat timber frame house in Cleveland Heights, not too far from my own place. It's a nice neighborhood, with a few chic bakeries and coffee shops dotted around the nearby streets. It's already dark when I arrive, but I can see the garden is well maintained, what there is of it in winter anyway. Marc has left the porch-light on, and I walk up the front steps as slowly as humanly possible.

The door opens before I have a chance to ring the bell. Marc's smile beams out at me, his teeth glistening in the lamplight. His hair has been slicked back. It looks … better like this. And he's wearing a cable knit sweater and dark jeans. Hardly a fashion statement, but definitely an improvement on the pin-stripe.

"You look nice," he says as he opens the door to invite me in.

"Thanks, you too," I say, surprised to find I mean it.

He helps me with my coat while I take in the surroundings. Someone's done a lot of work on this place. The floors are polished wood, and the picture frame windows are augmented with stylish navy drapes. The walls are painted in muted shades of cream. Something smells delicious too.

"Hope you like chicken," he says.

He loops my coat over an antique stand in the corner. I shiver at the loss of its warmth.

"Are you cold?" he asks, moving to the fireplace where he twists a knob and the flames leap higher. There's a comfy looking settee arranged at right angles to the hearth and an armchair across from it. They're upholstered in a navy fabric that matches the drapes. At the far end of the room is an intimate dining table set for two, a red candle flickering in the center and a single rose in a slim glass vase beside it.

"Can I get you a drink? I have beer, wine?"

"Water is fine," I say as I trail behind him to the kitchen, which is through a simple archway. The kitchen is small, but all the appliances are modern and stainless steel. Marc retrieves a couple of tumblers from the draining board and holds them under the ice dispenser in the refrigerator door, filling them with ice and cold water. He hands one to me and leans in to clink his glass against mine.

"Happy Valentine's Day," he says.

"You know this isn't a date, right?" I say awkwardly. "I mean, that email was only ..."

"I know, you're like Lacey and the others. Busy career girls. No time for serious relationships." His lips tighten into a grim line.

Busy career girls? What century is this guy from? I take a sip of my drink before I say anything. He's obviously gone to the trouble of cooking a nice dinner for us. That's something, right?

"I didn't mean anything," I say. "Only that we haven't known each other very long and just because it's Valentine's Day, I don't think we should feel ..." Nope, there's really no good way to finish that sentence.

"Pressured?" he suggests.

"Exactly." I sigh in relief, then remember the rose and the candle on the table. "I mean, I wouldn't want you to have a false impression of why I'm here."

"And why are you here exactly?" He leans in closer and I back away.

Because I accidentally sent you an email I meant to send to Lacey.

"Do you mind if I ask you a question?" he asks.

"I guess," I say, taking another sip of my water and moving through the archway toward the dining area. If we can get dinner underway, maybe we'll be able to steer the conversation into safer ground: food, or work, or something normal.

"Do you find your job fulfilling?" he asks.

"Yeah, I suppose. Why?"

"It seems like there are a lot of girls," he stops to correct himself, "women like you. Young, single, focused on their careers. And I wonder how much thought you give to what you're missing out on?"

"Like what?"

"Relationships, marriage, family." I open my mouth to protest, but he stills me with a gesture. "I'm only talking in the abstract, not about you in particular, but I go to those mingle events. I see how many more women there are than men."

And yet you still can't get a date. What does that tell you?

Wait a second. He does have a date. It's me.

"We're just busy. It's tough for us in the workplace," I say. "People talk about the glass ceiling being shattered, but it's still not easy being taken seriously in a law firm as a woman."

"Or is it that you don't really want to be taken seriously?" He's moving in closer again, but this time I don't step away. I take a deep breath and count to ten before I let him have it.

"How can you say something like that? You have no idea what it's like. You don't know me. You don't know the partners in my firm. Can you explain why in the 21st century in a firm with twenty-five partners, twenty-two of them are men? And that's not only my firm. Statistically -- "

"Hey, I'm sorry." Now he's backing away. "Why don't we talk about something else? I'll go get the appetizers. I hope you like bruschetta?"

My stomach grumbles. Loudly. Marc fails to stifle a grin. He beckons me to the table.

"Alright, I'm sorry too," I say. "It's been a long day."

"Official subject change. Computer games. I had a great idea about a new bonus level for ours."

He holds out a chair for me, and I sit. He leans over to lift my napkin and unfurls it with a flourish. It's the same blue as the upholstery and has been folded and ironed expertly. I wonder if he has a maid. He places the linen on my lap and presses his hand on my knee before removing it. Before I can say anything about it, he slips out to the kitchen where I hear him banging around with plates.

"Can I help?" I call out, twisting to see what he's doing.

"No need. Already done. Just warming in the oven." He appears in the archway with a plate of sinfully good-looking bruschetta topped with fresh tapenade. He bends to allow me to serve myself. The bread is warm and crusty. It smells divine. I only take one piece, but I'm sure I could eat the whole lot. My stomach growls again.

"You made these yourself?" I ask to cover it.

He places the plate down and seats himself across from me.

"I'm a man of many talents." He winks and slicks back his hair as he takes his seat.

Seriously, dude?

"So tell me about this new bonus level, for the game," I say in a desperate attempt to steer the conversation to safe ground.

"It's a take on D&D. The junior associate has to run the gauntlet while being chased by a fire-breathing dragon, wearing combustible armor."

This is even worse than the winking. Does he fantasize about female associates in combustible clothes?

"I don't think it should be a dragon," I say. "What about a judge? More realistic."

He rubs a thoughtful finger across his chin. "You might be right. How about Stewart?"

"I was thinking Mayhew," I say. "I went up before him for a T.R.O. yesterday. He chewed me out for using the wrong font in my brief."

"Poor baby."

The muscles in my neck stiffen.

"Sorry," Marc says. "I only meant that he's a ball-buster."

"And a sexist pig." *Just like you sounded a moment ago.*

"Do you want something else to drink?" Marc offers.

I can't help myself. "Maybe the new bonus level should be about castrating chauvinist judges, or male lawyers generally."

Marc gulps. "I might have a beer myself."

His voice is shaky as he stands up and moves to the kitchen. My knuckles tighten around my butter knife.

"You're a white girl, aren't you?" Marc calls from the other room.

I lift the knife without realizing I'm doing it until Marc reappears with a beer in one hand and a bottle of wine in the other.

"I have some chardonnay if you want some." He tilts the bottle toward my empty wine glass.

I drop the knife, embarrassed and reach for my glass.

"How did you know I liked chardonnay?" I ask.

"I remember from last time."

Last time?

"The mingle," he clarifies.

He pours the wine. I take a hesitant sip. It's not bad.

"Should go well with the chicken," he says as he takes his seat and opens his beer. He pours it into his wine glass before raising it to me. "Salut."

"Slàinte," I say, raising my own glass.

"Closet *Outlander* fan?"

My cheeks blaze when I realize I must have picked up the Gaelic toast from my obsession with the time traveling romance. Is Marc a fan too? Ick.

"You like *Game of Thrones* too?" he asks as he lifts his beer for another sip.

"You seriously watch that rubbish?"

"Only for the dragons." A boyish grin lights his eyes. In the candlelight, I notice gold flecks dancing around his pupils.

Get a grip, Hannah.

This. Is. Not. A. Date.

"When do you have time for all this extra-curricular stuff anyway?" I ask him. "Aren't you on the partnership track too?"

"If something's worth doing, I make time." He locks his eyes with mine. It feels like a contest. I look away first. He taps the back of my hand where it's resting on the table. "Ready for what's coming next?"

I yank my hand away from him.

"I only meant the next course, Hannah. You're so jumpy."

Flustered, I place my napkin on the table and reach for his plate. "Let me help you clear these."

He waves me aside.

"No way. You're my date." A flash of panic sparks across his face and he corrects himself. "My guest."

He collects the plates and bustles into the kitchen. I let out a relieved breath. This is only supposed to be friends having a casual dinner. It wasn't even supposed to be that. I only accepted the invitation by mistake.

"Are you a leg or a breast gal?" he calls out.

My mouth drops open but then I realize he means the chicken.

"Either's fine." I grab for my wineglass and drain it, wondering if I should have more while he's out of the room. Instead, I reach for the remains of my water and chug it down too, spluttering as I take in too much.

"You alright?" he calls.

I thump myself on the chest.

"Yes," I rasp. "Water went down the wrong way."

He's in the archway with an icy pitcher which he places on the table in front of me. "Do you need some more?"

"Thanks."

I pour some out and drink it more slowly, letting it soothe my nerves. He pats my shoulder and returns to the kitchen. My skin shivers where he touched it. And they're not necessarily bad shivers either.

Get a grip, Hannah! This is Marc. *Marc-Marc. Just friends Marc.*

PIN-STRIPE SUIT MARC, for the love of all that's Holy.

But he's not wearing pin-stripes tonight ….

My phone beeps in my pocket. It's a text from Lacey: *You give in to his charms yet?*

Heat flames up my neck. I type out a quick reply: *When pigs fly.*

"Something wrong?" Marc appears with two plates laden with roast chicken and all the trimmings. There are even slices of bacon browned on top. "Hope you like a good old-fashioned roast. Decided to stick with the classics tonight."

He places my plate in front of me and a hint of rosemary wafts through the air. My stomach gurgles again, and I blush, covering my face with my hands.

He smiles. His teeth are white and even. "Best compliment a chef could ask for." Then he leans over, obviously trying to get a look at my phone screen. I replace it in my pocket before he can read it.

"Problem at work?" he asks.

"No, it's … nothing. It's not important," I say. "This looks delicious."

He takes his place, setting his own dinner in front of him.

I raise a slice of bacon to my mouth. The texture is the perfect blend of meatiness and crispiness. "Hey, how did you know I'm not Jewish or something?" I ask.

"You were eating a bacon-wrapped shrimp at the mingle," he says.

Ugh. Why does he have to say stuff like that? Coming from another guy it might sound like a compliment, but the way I remember him that night, it just makes him seem creepy. I crunch down my bacon.

We eat for a while in silence and the food tastes as good as it looks. When we're done, Marc offers me seconds.

"I honestly couldn't eat another thing," I say, patting my very contented stomach.

"Not even the chocolate-covered strawberries I made for dessert?"

"You didn't, seriously? I thought this wasn't a *date* date."

He looks away and then pushes his plate to the side. His mouth forms into a line again.

Shit. I'm being such a bitch, after he cooked me a nice dinner.

"Marc, the meal was wonderful. Seriously," I say. "I'm just really full."

He reaches for the chardonnay, tilting it toward me. "Refill?"

"No, thanks. I shouldn't. I'm driving tonight."

"You don't have to."

What? He better not be saying what I think he's saying.

"I mean, you could sleep on the sofa, if you wanted to." He nods to the comfy couch by the fire.

Oh. That's still bad, but not as bad as I was thinking. And that sofa does look pretty inviting, compared to braving the chill air outside. And compared to my messy bedsit with three days' worth of breakfast dishes piled in the sink and a ratty old space heater that clunks and whines all night.

Get it together, Hannah. The car's only half a block down the street.

"We could sit over there now if you like," he says. "It's more comfortable than it looks."

It looks plenty comfortable. That's the problem.

"I'm fine here, thanks." I cross my arms over my chest. Classic defensive posture, but I can't help it.

"Can I ask you something?" he asks, his eyes narrowing.

"Only if it's about our computer game," I say.

"Kind of," he says. "Where do you see yourself in ten years?"

Yeah, do more of the career girl stuff. That will get me out of here.

"The newest partner at my firm, of course." I force a chuckle, but it sounds like a groan.

"Of course." His laughter sounds forced too and his accompanying smile doesn't reach his eyes. "But what about family?"

"I'm an only child," I say.

"Not *that* family. I meant a family of your own."

"Marc, I – "

"Wait, hear me out. Just for a moment, pretend this isn't like alien territory for you." He seems so earnest, I almost hate to cut him off, but I have to.

"Aliens. Now there's a good idea for a bonus level," I say in a meek attempt at humor.

"Don't you want to get married, have kids?" He plows on, undeterred by my unfunny joke. "All we ever seem to talk about in our emails is the partnership track."

"It's important to me."

"Isn't anything else important to you? Why do you even go to the mingles if you don't want to meet someone?"

"Marc, I'm sorry, but I really should be going."

"Wait." He reaches across the table for my hand but I draw back, pushing my chair away from the table. "Seriously, do all you girls really want to wake up at forty and find you've got nothing but work in your lives? How old are you now anyway?"

This time I do stand up and move behind my chair, using it as a barrier between us. He moves to stand as well, but I motion him down again with a gesture that looks almost like shaking a fist. I grip the chair and watch as my knuckles turn white.

"Marc, I'm going to give you some free advice here because you cooked me dinner and despite everything I think you're a nice guy."

He opens his mouth but I glare him into silence.

"First, never ask a lady her age. It's rude, in case no one's ever told you. Second, plenty of men care more about their careers than anything else, and no one ever questions them. And third, if you want a date, try to be less obvious and," I wave my hands searching for the right word, "weird about it."

My chest heaves. My arms lock against the chair. Marc looks as if I've slapped him and I feel like the most ungrateful bitch in the universe, but it had to be said.

Didn't it?

He stares at the candle, not meeting my eyes.

"You're right. I'm sorry. You should go," he says as he slowly stands and collects the plates. Mine is almost completely clean. I've eaten everything and had more wine than I can obviously handle.

"At least let me help you." I reach for the empty glasses.

"No, you should go," he repeats. "I'll take care of it."

He heads for the kitchen and I'm left alone. The only noise is the fire crackling. That's when I realize he's turned off the soft music that had been playing in the background. I hadn't even noticed it until it was gone.

My cellphone buzzes again.

Lacey's new text reads: *Pigs flying yet?*

More like Hell freezing over. I put the phone back into my pocket without answering.

I can't leave without making this right. I move to the kitchen archway.

"Marc?" I say softly. He's rinsing the plates. He doesn't turn to look at me. "Marc, please, I'm sorry. Can we talk?"

This time, he does look up and his eyes are sheened over. "It's okay. I get it. I know I come on a bit strong. You should go."

"No, really, come and sit. Let me talk to you."

"What about?" he asks.

"I think you're a nice guy, and I think you honestly could be a good date. You're certainly a good cook."

That gets a small smile out of him.

I tilt my head toward the living area. "C'mon. Let's talk. Friends?"

He drops the dish he's holding into a sink full of soapy water and reaches for a kitchen towel to dry his hands. "Should I bring the chocolate covered strawberries?" he asks.

I sigh. "Sure, why not?"

A few minutes later we're settled by the fire, me on the sofa and him in the armchair, a platter of sinfully amazing chocolate covered strawberries between us on the coffee table.

"You really went to a lot of trouble tonight," I say. "Thanks."

"It was nothing. I like to cook."

If only he was the woman here, and I was the guy, this scenario could really work out.

"You're very good at it," I say.

"Thanks." A hint of crimson flares through his cheeks. It's actually pretty cute, kind of boyish.

"But ..."

He looks up at me with those hazel-flecked eyes. "There's always a *but* with you girls, isn't there?"

"Well, that's your problem right there. All this stuff with the *you career girls*. This isn't the 1950s. It's insulting."

"But girls today seem to be only interested in work, at least all the girls I meet, even the ones at those mingles. I mean, why *do* you go to them if you don't want to meet guys?"

"We *do* want to meet guys, only not ..."

"Not guys like me?"

"I didn't say that."

"That's what you meant, though."

"Well, why do *you* go to those mingles if you only want a housewife? They're young *professional* gatherings, meaning the women there are professionals too."

"I like smart women."

"Huh?"

"I like women like you, women with ambition, with more going on up here," he taps his temple, "than babies and weddings."

I shake my head. "Okay, I'm lost."

"I don't want a partner who only wants a family, or who only wants a career."

"Oh."

"I want both. Don't you?" he asks, peering at me intently.

"Of course." But do I really? I mean, I only went to that mingle in the first place because my sister and mother pressured me. There has to be something else, though, doesn't there?

"Maybe I need professional help," I say as a half-joke.

"Maybe you need another one of these." He passes me another chocolate covered strawberry, and I take it willingly, letting the chocolate slowly melt in my mouth.

"Hey, tell me something about yourself," he says, "something I don't know, something not about work *and* not about marriage or babies."

"Okay, um, well, I really like lizards."

He raises both eyebrows and an adorable little "v" forms between his eyes. I almost want to smooth it out with my thumb.

"Seriously," I say. "I used to have a monitor lizard when I was a child. I called him Slimy even though his scales were actually rough. I was very young when I got him, and I couldn't think of a better name."

Marc squints with one eye, sizing me up.

"What?" I ask.

"Nothing," he says. "It just explains a lot."

I can't help it. I grab a throw pillow and hurl it at him.

"So, you tell me something about you, something that I don't know," I say. "And not something icky."

He scowls at me and then glances out the window before answering.

"Okay. How about … I read hands."

"You mean like fortune telling?" I ask.

"Guilty as charged."

I laugh and reach for another strawberry.

"Hey," he says. "Do you want me to read you?"

I pause with the strawberry halfway to my mouth. "See? That's actually a little icky, Marc."

"Seriously," he says. "I really do know how to read palms. I took a course at college on the occult and all sorts of other superstitions."

"What college was that?"

"Well, it was more of a summer school program."

"A likely story," I say before biting into the strawberry. I groan in pleasure. "These things are amazing," I say with my mouth half-full. "Where do you get the chocolate?"

"I make it myself."

"Get out of here!"

"I really do. Mom taught me. When I was a kid."

"How do you make it?"

"Family secret. If I told you, I'd have to kill you."

"If you tell me, I'll let you read my palm."

What am I doing? Am I actually flirting with him?

"If I tell you, will you let me read your palm and have a glass of ice wine with me? I have a great bottle chilling in the fridge."

"I love ice wine." Why did he have to go there? Ice wine is my downfall. My most major downfall. And it's perfect with chocolate covered strawberries.

"Stay right there." Marc is on his feet and heading for the kitchen before I can think of anything else to say.

My cellphone buzzes again and I reach for it.

Lacey has texted: *Inquiring minds want to know … pigs flying?*

I listen to Marc clattering around in the kitchen. I pop another strawberry in my mouth and type: *Preparing for lift-off. Will send S.O.S. if we crash and burn.*

Salt to a Wound
Mandy Broughton

I PLOPPED a mound of faux food onto the tray offered before me. Meatloaf—it was a pale comparison to my homemade delicacy. As to the bearer of the tray, I didn't have to observe the recipient's half grown beard that wasn't fashionably rugged, his smell told me all I needed to know. I wrinkled my nose at the body odor.

He caught me staring. "Community service?"

"How did you know?" I pushed the hairnet off my forehead. I feared I had smudged what had once been delicately painted eyebrows.

Don't strike me as natural." He grinned, showing his tooth. "And the shoes." He pointed a gnarled finger at my Louboutins.

I frowned, shifting my weight on said designer shoes. "It doesn't hurt to look good while I'm doing my part to battle... homelessness," I said. "But I really expected a PR job. This standing all day, it's not really for the people like me."

He laughed, a deep gurgling guffaw. "You don't like us. You care only about yourself." He stood there, hunchbacked and smelly. No one behind him and no one to hold up. The last to serve. And he demanded from me what I didn't want to give. My attention.

"What'd you do?" he asked, smearing spittle across his beard.

I glanced to my left to catch a particular eavesdropper. He wasn't there. "I didn't do a thing," I said. "I only wanted to impress a man on our first date."

***

"Did you add salt to the meatloaf?" Dyll, the non-cooking expert asked. He swept his hand across his forehead, brushing his curly dark locks to the side. He was the love of my life; he just didn't know it yet.

I melted. He'd finally agreed to a date. I knew he couldn't resist my feminine wiles once we went out. That's why he'd held off for so long. Months of playing cat and mouse, well, now the mouse was eating at my downtown loft apartment.

"Why do you ask, sweetie?" I touched my lacy napkin to the corners of my mouth, trying to regain control of my racing heart.

"It needs salt."

"It doesn't need salt." I placed another forkful in my mouth, gently. Mustn't muss my lipstick. "I followed the recipe exactly."

"What happened to your cook?" Dyll pushed the repast away from him as if it were distasteful. "You forgot the salt."

"I didn't forget," I said, swallowing. I fingered my Waterford tea glass. "You said you wanted a woman who takes care of herself. Women who take care of themselves make meatloaf. So I gave Marjorie the day off. Isn't it delicious? I can cook and look this good."

"When you deign to make meatloaf, add salt to it." He dared to point his fork at me.

"I'm sorry, when did you go to culinary school?" I chewed another delicious forkful.

"I've been eating all my life," Dyll said. "I know what meatloaf tastes like."

"Really? I thought you were heir to The Foundation. When did you eat meatloaf?"

Dyll kicked his chair back. "My father wanted us to be in touch with the little people. He takes our *noblesse oblige* seriously but felt we weren't doing the same. One day, in a fit of anger, he instructed our chef to use Kobe beef and make meatloaf." He tapped his manly manicured nails across my Armani Casa table. "So I know what meatloaf tastes like."

I slid him a sly smile. I wondered if I needed to touch up my lipstick. "And what does it taste like?"

"This," he said, pointing his fork at the white and blue Wedgwood dinner plate, "with salt."

I started to answer him but looked at my security monitor instead. Taking the casserole dish, I dashed into the hall. Dashed as well as I could in my new sling backs. Dyll easily overtook me, carrying his fork, and demanded to know where I was taking his supper.

I called to my sometime partner in crime, Safron. She had just begun the powerwalking craze and had exited the elevator on my floor. Cradling her Yorkie, Pepita, she stopped.

"KaiAnne!" Safron threw manicured hands up giving air hugs and kisses. "Love the new shoes, but you shouldn't wear them walking." She narrowed her eyelids as much as her false eyelashes would allow. "How's the date with that hunk of a man?"

"It'd be nicer if we could eat," he said.

"What do you think of this?" I showed her my meatloaf.

"Are you making homemade dog food again?" Safron let Pepita have a sniff. "You know Pepita is a vegan."

"It's our dinner. I made it for Dyll. He wanted a woman who can take care of herself."

"And you cooked?" Safron asked. Pepita looked interested. "Darling, that's so sweet!"

"Sweet?!" Dyll loomed, casting his dark cloud about us. I preferred the stormy cloud harassing others, not me. "It's not sweet when my dear date feels the need to lie to me."

"By calling it dinner?" Safron asked.

"No," Dyll said, handing her his fork, "by saying it has salt. Do you taste salt?"

Safron backed away from the casserole, her eyes wide. She refused to take the fork. "I would love to help but I've just started detox. No 'b' foods today."

"It's meatloaf." I pushed it closer to her.

"No beef." Safron smiled, said something inane and powerwalked off, carrying her dog. Pepita whimpered as she looked over Safron's shoulder. The longing in her eyes told me she wanted to try my meatloaf.

Dyll grabbed the dish from me. I teetered down the hallway and just barely made it to the elevator. "Darling, must we fuss on our first date?"

"If you feel the need to torture me with food, yes, yes, we must fuss." He sniffed the dish and pulled it away quickly from his nose. "If you and I get married, and our chef falls ill, how will I survive?"

"I can use the phone. I order dinner all the time."

Dyll grunted. "And if your cell phone battery goes dead?"

I sighed, "Really, you are being unreasonable."

"Unreasonable? This food is inedible."

"It's meatloaf," I said, looking in the elevator's mirrored walls. Not a hair out of place, I touched my perfect coiffure. I smiled, "It's what the regular people eat. Slumming on our first date, isn't that exciting?" He grunted again, I thought it was rather unbecoming.

We exited the garage level. He climbed into the Benz and demanded I get in, without even holding the door for me.

***

"That nice man said it tasted great," I leaned back in my seat. Dyll and I had just left the supermarket. Taste testing. We had four responses before the store manager asked us to vacate the premises.

"He couldn't keep his eyes off your chest." Dyll shifted gears. "The two ladies agreed with me. Needs salt."

"The nice young man loved it."

"College student," Dyll said. "He's two steps away from homelessness. He'd say anything for a free meal. Did you see him sneak back for seconds?"

"Because he loved it."

"Because he's starving. Besides, it needs salt." Grinding the gears, Dyll shifted again. "And you didn't add salt. I can prove it."

Crossing my arms, I tapped a French manicured nail on my bicep. "I added salt. And just how are you going to disprove it?"

Dyll turned off the main road.

"Merle's?" I sat up straighter. "We have reservations?"

"No, of course not. My standing reservation is on Tuesdays." Dyll hopped out of the car and grabbed the meatloaf from the floorboard. An attendant opened the door for me. I smiled at him and slowly unfolded out of the car. He fell over himself, trying to help me out. "Do you like meatloaf?" I asked.

"I love meatloaf," he stammered.

I grinned. "See, another one loves my meatloaf."

Dyll paused by the glass door. "That doesn't prove anything, he hasn't even tasted it."

I gave the sweet attendant a small wave. Dyll barged into the restaurant with the dish, leaving the car with the blushing young man. By the time I caught up with him, he was demanding to see the head chef.

"Chef Merle!" I waved as I saw my favorite chef rounding the tables, greeting his customers. I always ate his veal medallions on Mondays. Takeout. "I can use the phone to order," I muttered.

The ancient chef smiled and came to greet us but recoiled when Dyll showed him my meatloaf. "Does this need salt?" Dyll demanded.

"I added salt." I learned forward to show more cleavage for Merle to admire. Chef Merle always said I was his favorite customer.

"She did not." Dyll stepped in front of me, closing the gap between him and Chef Merle. "And you're going to confirm it."

***

The homeless man stood in awe. "And he called the police on you?"

"Only after KaiAnne shoved the meatloaf into his mouth," a new voice said. Dyll stood to my left. Drat. He had overheard us after all. Dark. Brooding. And deliciously handsome.

I licked my lips. "You're the one who held him down," I said.

"You forgot the salt." Dyll raised the serving spoon as if it were a sword. "That's the bigger crime."

The homeless man looked at him and then me. He took his tray and sped away. I grinned at my love. Maybe after our thirty hours of community service, I could convince him to go on a second date. I'd been practicing baking. Maybe I'd bake him a pie. And I'd make sure I use *sugar* this time, not salt. It's hard when they're both white.

Dyll huffed. I squinted my eye, knowing how irresistible I was and then gave him my coy look. His cheeks turned pink.

"Let's go," he said softly. He held out a hand to me.

We started to leave the serving line when one more customer darted in, clutching his tray.

"Meatloaf," he said, eying the mound of mush in front of me. "Does it have enough salt?"

I twirled the serving spoon in my right hand, squeezed Dyll's hand in my left and uttered the truest words ever, "I added it myself."

Dyll dropped my hand, took a forkful, and plopped it into his mouth. He chewed thoughtfully then frowned. "It needs pepper."

Speed Freaks
Monica Shaughnessy

I DON'T date. I'm not into wearing high heels and lipstick or feigning interest in small talk. I'm just not. Hook-ups are easier. No one has to pretend to be anything other than a quick lay, and that's the way I like it. My mother, on the other hand, is convinced I'm an old maid at twenty-seven, convinced she will die grandchildless. At her insistence, I'm at Chez Vino, a cheesy circa-1990s wine bar, counting cars on Interstate 45 as they crawl by during evening rush hour. I scan the dark room while I wait for my dates to arrive. I am one of ten women, and we're seated in a long row of two-top tables. They are the gorgeous perfume counter girls with meticulously applied eye shadow, and I am the frumpy shopper. My mother's voice echoes in my head, "Would it kill you to brush your hair, dear? Put on a little mascara?"

"Thank you for joining us, Houston singles!" Ms. Henley, the event's organizer, says into a microphone. Blue pantsuit, unnaturally smooth forehead, pink nails. She does spin class with my mother, so I couldn't ditch tonight and lie about it later, which is what I hoped to do from the first mention of *find you a husband*. "You have five minutes to get to know each other. Your time ends when I say 'switch.' This will seem very short for some of your dates and very looong for others." She waits for the chuckles to die down. "Let the speed dating begin!"

Number One, a guy that could double for the hipster in the old Apple Computer commercials, sits at my table. Four o'clock shadow? Check. Ironic cardigan? Check. He swipes his dark bangs to one side and smiles. "Hey, I'm Grant."

"Hey," I say, pointing to his nametag, "I know."

Number One laughs, all "shucks ma'am," and blushes. "Sorry. Let's start over,"—he scans the sticker on my shirt—"Lindsey."

"Sure. Why not?" I casually take out my phone, open Evernote, and tap into the "Speed Freaks" notebook. Why not? I keep track of everything else, including which Bucky's barista gives me the highest whip on my foam.

"You're not going to believe this," Grant says, "but I own that shirt." He points to my "Free

Mustache Rides" t-shirt. "I only wear it right after I shave, though. Otherwise, it's not—"

"Ironic?"

"Yeah." He clears his throat. "So I'm a programmer," he says. "JavaScript." All I notice are his eyebrows. Several tiny hairs jut out of place. "What do you do?"

Is tonight a good time for the truth? Is any night? Nah. "I'm a professional bikini waxer. I rip hair off of women's—"

"I got it. No need to explain." Number One thinks a moment. "Do you, um, like your job?" He rests his elbows on the table. "That seems a little inappropriate for me to ask, though. Considering."

"I love my job." I toss my hair over my shoulder. "Love. It."

He has nowhere to go with this. "I like your phone," he finally says.

"Of course you do, hipster dude. It's an *Apple* iPhone."

Number One frowns. "I don't get it."

"Switch!" Ms. Henley shouts. The mic squeals.

As soon as my first date leaves, I make a note of him on my phone. *Number One: Mr. Ironic.* When Number Two slides into the opposite chair, I question my decision to abstain from alcohol this evening. He is blond and gorgeous, and I hate him already. I dispense with the chitchat and get right to the heart of the matter. "Did you date a cheerleader in high school?"

He blinks, flustered. "Yes."

"The head cheerleader?"

"Yes." A smile creeps across his overly symmetrical face. He's beginning to enjoy my line of questioning. "Were you a cheerleader, Lindsey?" He bumps my knee with his.

"Do I *look* like I was a cheerleader?"

He rubs his chiseled chin. "No, but I bet you were on drill team. You have the legs for it."

"Seriously? You can't even see under the table. And besides, I'm wearing jeans." I wave madly at the ginger-haired bartender. A nod. A few seconds later, a waitress appears and takes my whiskey sour order.

"Switch!"

I tap notes into my phone. *Number Two: full of number two.*

Number Three arrives, along with my drink. Good God. I tell the waitress to keep my tab open, wide open. Before speaking, I count the lines on his forehead like I'm counting the rings of a tree. "I thought this was supposed to be a Millennial Event," I say to him.

"I am a Millennial," he says.

"What millennium?" I ask.

He narrows his eyes, flashing crow's feet. Hasn't this guy heard of sunscreen? "A Millennial is anyone born between the early 1980s to the early 2000s. I was born in 1980." He sits back and dusts lint from his wool blazer. "I'm barely in, but I made it."

"You sure about that?" I tip the last of my whiskey sour and shake the glass. The dream-come-true behind the bar catches my drift and pours me another. I let the clock run out on Number Three, keeping my eyes to the window. Ms. Henley is totally right. Five minutes is an eternity with the wrong person. *Wool blazer*, I type after he leaves.

Number Four is younger, maybe a year older than me. He's tall, tall enough to hit his head on the pendant lamp, and he's got big brown eyes. Okay, I admit I'm jealous of his coal-black hair. Mine is dark, too, but it's more the color of mud. For the first time tonight, I'm paying attention. He's the kind of guy my mother would grab in the grocery store and shove in front of me. "Look, Lindsey, here's a nice one," she'd say, as if we were picking out melons. "Feel his arm." I tell you this only because it happened last week. True story.

He shakes my hand. "Nice to meet you, Lindsey," he says. His deep voice tickles my inner ear. I detect a slight Hispanic accent.

"Nice to meet you, Marco." I cross my arms over my ironic t-shirt. Fine, it's ironic. "Tell me the truth," I say. "How many women have said 'polo' to you tonight?"

"Three." His teeth are the color of Polar Ice gum. To my surprise, I imagine them biting my neck. Okay, I'm clearly confused.

"Then I won't make it four. What do you do for a living?" I ask. I am officially a dork.

"I'm the bar-back at Tango."

"I love that place." I study him a moment. "Wait. You're one of the dancers, right? One of the guys who tangos with women from the crowd? I think I've seen you."

"You may have even danced with me," he says with a wink.

"No. I think I'd remember that." I toy with my empty glass, wetting my fingers on the condensation. "That place is a meat market. Am I right?"

"Yes, and I'm the side of beef." His eyes grow dull. I've hit a nerve.

"Disgusting the way women act sometimes," I say.

"Men act that way all the time." He shrugs. "It's a job. A good paying job. As long as I don't take it seriously, everything's fine. In a year, I'll be out of culinary school and into a good kitchen. I hope." He leans back against his chair. "I won't look like this forever."

I want to scream, "No, no, no! You will be gorgeous until you're eighty! And even then, old hags will crawl across the nursing home just to touch your thigh." Instead, I say, "Yeah, me neither." What can I say? I'm a sucker for good genes. "So what brings you to this whole speed dating—"

"Switch!"

I'm a little relieved. Ms. Henley has saved me from at least six months of frantic soul-searching. I glance at the bartender and make eye contact. No, I don't want a drink. Can you guess what I want? A minute later, the waitress brings my third whiskey sour of the evening. The bartender is a bad guesser.

"Hi, I'm Billy," Number Five says.

"Shhhhhh," I say to him. I've forgotten to make notes, so I do so now. *Number Four: Marco...Polo!* I glance across the table. *Number Five: I'm Billy.* Come on. With a name like that, the guy never had a chance.

The next four dates pass like childbirth, a pain I am not familiar with but one my mother recounts when I disappoint her. Like tonight.

Number Six: Sasquatch. No need to look further, folks. I found him.

Number Seven: Barely Hairly. When you start seeing scalp, my brotha, you gotta go for it. Shave it bald. Just sayin'.

Number Eight: Budweiser. Next.

Number Nine: Marathon Man. No, I don't need you to tell me you like running. It's obvious from your rail-thin body, your leathered face, and your freaking 26.2 t-shirt. But congratulate yourself because you just motivated *me* to run. In the other direction.

During this time, I flirt with the bartender, throwing mischievous looks across the bar. Red hair drives me crazy. Absolutely crazy. And those arms. Strong, but not overly masculine, and covered with sleeve tats. I picture them around my waist, pulling me closer, closer, our hips touching. I chew on my stir straw. What's that? A smile? A wink?

Blue Pantsuit interrupts my flow. "Switch!" she yells.

Number Ten drops into the seat across from me. And he has a mustache. Great.

"I love your shirt," he says to me. "Just love it." His green button-down oxford deepens the emerald of his eyes. He's raked his dirty blond hair slightly forward to give the impression he didn't spend too much time on it when I know damn well he did.

I toss my straw and place my elbows on the table. "Sure you're in the right place?"

"Of course I'm in the right place," he says.

"Hey, look, it's cool with me. I'm not passing judgment. But this event seems a little…hetero for you."

He studies me a moment. Then his shoulders relax. "It was my mother's idea. She's still so clueless."

I pat his hand. "She'll figure it out one day. But you're a good boy for humoring her." I lower my voice. "A bunch of freaks tonight. Am I right?"

"Oh, I wouldn't say that." He smiles wryly. "I'm going home with at least one match."

I grab his hands and squeeze. "Who? Who?"

"Marco."

"Freaking polo," I say. "I didn't catch it, and my gay-dar is topnotch."

He laughs. "Mine's better. A lot better."

I glance across the bar and find the bartender staring at me. I blush for the first time tonight.

"That concludes our evening, speed daters," Ms. Henley says. Her features remain motionless as she talks. "Go home and score your favorites online. If anyone marks you as a favorite, too, then you're a match. I'll let you know the results in a couple of days." She blathers on about details that don't matter to me.

I glance at Number Ten's nametag. "Listen, Scott, I don't want to be rude, but I've got a match of my own to make." I nod toward the bartender.

He turns and looks in the direction of my gaze. "I knew you were in the wrong place, too. Took me a minute, but I figured it out." He slaps me on the shoulder. "Your redhead is red hot. If you don't come back with her number, I'm going to be very disappointed."

"Me, too. Just don't tell my mother."

Prima Facie

Artemis Greenleaf

EMILY COMBED her hair for the third time in fifteen minutes. Earlier in the day, she toyed with the idea of canceling the dinner, but Susan had been so insistent that her cousin, Nick, was absolutely perfect for her that she finally gave in and let her friend arrange the date. Now, Emily was going to meet him at The Orange Penguin in half an hour.

She tossed her purse into the passenger's seat and got in the car. What if he was perfect for her? Was she ready for a relationship? She'd just graduated from law school and was still looking for a job. Was it a good idea to start a relationship with the 'perfect' guy at the same time? Then again, maybe he wouldn't be Mr. Right, but he might be Mr. Right Now.

The Orange Penguin was nothing fancy, one of the last remaining outposts of a once-popular chain. It had been years since she'd eaten there - she hadn't even realized that the place was still open until Nick suggested meeting there. But the food was both good and inexpensive, which appealed to Emily. She insisted on paying her own way and wasn't exactly flush with cash.

Nick had told her that he was 6'4" and would be wearing a blue polo. She arrived ten minutes early, hoping to observe him for a minute or two before introducing herself.

Apparently, he had the same idea. There was a tall man in a blue polo sitting on one of the concrete benches in front of the restaurant, playing with his cell phone.

She scanned him from head to toe. He looked like a gym rat – lots of muscle (but not too much), and military style, close-cropped hair. *At least he's easy on the eyes.* "Hello?" Emily asked as she approached. "Are you Nick?"

He stood up. "Emily?"

"That's me." She held out her hand, business-like, for a handshake. She'd been on six job interviews this week, and she couldn't help herself.

As they went into the restaurant, Emily noticed that he had 'the walk' – a certain bearing that was somewhere between confidence and swagger that was common to military and law enforcement personnel. Before her father became a truck driver, he had been a Marine. Even with half his leg amputated, he still had it.

They were seated at a table near the window in the middle of the dining room. The server had just left with their orders, and Emily dreaded the small talk that would fill the time until the food came.

The hostess led three nondescript men past them. One wore a scraggly attempt at a beard, one wore a stained 'I'm with Stupid' tee-shirt, and the last one was in dire need of shampoo. Emily crinkled her nose, and her eyes followed the new diners to their table, two away from hers and Nick's.

"What's wrong?" Nick asked.

"Do you smell that?" Emily whispered.

He took a whiff. "Acetone." He gave the trio a sidelong glance.

Emily nodded. "I don't trust people who smell like nail polish remover."

"Agreed," said Nick.

Emily could tell he was sizing her up, trying to make sense of her, trying to puzzle out what she knew. And she let him keep working at it. *Always leave them wanting more*, her mother liked to say.

"Have you been here before?" she asked.

"Once or twice." He smiled at her, then his eyes darted to the three men.

Emily tracked them with her peripheral vision. As the man in the middle of the group, the bearded one, opened his menu, he screamed. Nick stood up, his right hand hovered near his hip, then dropped.

I knew it. Cop. Gun's in his car. Score one for the summer internship at the DA's office.

"Get them off me! Get them off!" The bearded man at the other table leaped to his feet and flung the menu to the ground, stomping on it. His bony hands raked at his chest and shoulders as he screamed again.

"Dude!" 'I'm-With-Stupid' said. "What is with you?"

"You did this! You're one of them! Why are you trying to kill me, Justin?" he sobbed.

"What are you talking about? I'm not trying to kill you," Justin replied.

"Don't. Lie. To. Me," the man bellowed. He grabbed at his friend.

Greasy hair tried to interfere. "Tony! Stop it!"

Emily was relieved that Nick wasn't testosterone-addled macho man, dumb enough to rush into the middle of that fight – three against one, no tools, and no backup. He did, however, move in front of her, and she had to peer around him to see what was going on.

Tony picked up the interloper and hurled him against the window. The thick glass didn't break, but the man's head thudded hard against it. He slithered to the floor, where he sat and tried to shake off the cobwebs.

Restaurant patrons began screaming and running, tripping over chairs and each other after what had been an amusing sideshow turned to violent chaos. Before she could get up to evacuate, Emily's chair was knocked over, and she scrambled under the table to keep from being trampled. Nick bent to help her up, but the last surge of panicked diners up-ended the table and trapped him underneath it. Emily pulled at the solid oak, family-sized table trying to free him. It took a few moments before he started pushing on it. A few good tugs had gotten the table mostly off of him – two thirds or so of it rested on the floor, and the rest covered his abdomen and thighs.

Tony, chest heaving, saw what they were trying to do, and roared over, standing on the table. "What are you trying to do to my mother?" he demanded. He failed to notice that his friends had taken that opportunity to bolt for the exit.

Nick stopped struggling, to conserve his energy, perhaps.

Emily backed away slowly. When her chair had tipped over, her purse fell, and most of her belongings were scattered over the stained carpet. She spotted her cell phone about ten feet away and eased toward it.

"Mama?" Tony blubbered. "You're not leaving me are you?"

"No, baby," she replied. "Mama's not leaving you. I just need to get something."

She glanced at Nick, who was struggling for air. Slowly, deliberately, she picked up her phone. *I can do this*. "Tony, did you take something before you came here?" She advanced slowly.

Tony stepped off the table and Nick sucked in a huge breath.

"Yes, Mama," Tony hung his head.

Her eyes flicked down to her phone from time to time as she talked. Emily's hands shook, and it was hard to tap the right live tiles on the screen. "Tony, it's okay. Focus on the sound of my voice and take a deep breath." Meditation music started playing from her smartphone.

Tony did as he was told. Nick freed himself from the table, but didn't get up. His left leg was bent weirdly, and Emily wondered if it was broken.

She brushed his shoulder with her foot, then stood between him and Tony. *Hold on, Nick.* "Tony, take another deep breath, but this time, hold it for about five seconds. Can you do that for me?" *We should all try this.*

Tony complied. Sweat soaked his tee-shirt and glistened on his forehead.

"Okay, Tony. Thank you. You took something before you came here. What was it? Angel Dust?" *You think you're the first duster to have a bad trip? Please.*

His eyes narrowed. "Why you want to know?"

"Because you're having a bad trip. None of the things you see are real. I want the doctors to know how to help you."

"I don't need no damn doctors!" Spittle flew from his lips, and he picked up a chair. "The spiders ain't real?"

"No, Tony. They're just in your head."

"Then you ain't my Mama, neither."

"No Tony, I'm not. But I do care what happens to you."

He glowered. But he set the chair back on the floor.

"Listen to me, Tony. I'm sure several of the people outside have already called 911. The police will come, and if you're acting all crazy, you're going to get shot. Do you want to leave here in a body bag, Tony? How would your mother feel if she had to bury you?"

He sat on the floor. Tears started and he cried like a small child who didn't get that candy bar in the grocery checkout line.

"You're going to be okay. When the PCP wears off, you won't see the spiders anymore. But you might be able to get them to go away sooner."

"How?" he sobbed.

"These spiders are night creatures, right? They like the dark. So think of yourself as a glowing white light. You hurt their eyes, so they run away."

Emily glanced at her phone. The battery charge indicator was in the red zone. *Hurry up, EMS.*

The police came, entering dramatically, but Tony went meekly out to the ambulance with them, muttering to himself about grasshoppers and vanilla.

Emily closed her eyes as she took a deep breath and exhaled slowly. She didn't pay any attention to the officers establishing a perimeter or the static-y radio chatter.

She frowned at the quickly coloring goose egg above his left eye. "That's quite a bump on your head. Are you okay?" she asked Nick.

"Mostly," he replied.

He tried to sit up and she gently pushed him back down. "You might have internal injuries.

Lie still." She left her hand on his chest. Just to make sure.

He looked up at her and shook his head. "You were amazing. I've never seen anybody talk a dust head down like that."

Emily studied his face, trying to decide how much to tell him. "I spent a lot of time working on crisis intervention hotlines in college."

Nick nodded. "Interesting choice. Somehow, that doesn't surprise me."

Emily picked an imaginary bit of debris off his collar "I lost…a very close friend to suicide." It had been almost three years since Kyle had used a pistol to paint the wall of his dorm with his brains, but the wound was still raw.

"Benson?" the officer who had just walked up interrupted.

"Hey, Garcia," Nick replied.

"There's a second EMS on the way. What happened?"

Nick rolled his eyes. "Just another dust head freakout. Man, I'd rather deal with tweakers."

Garcia laughed.

Paramedics came through the door with a stretcher for Nick and started their injury assessment.

An officer with a clipboard approached Emily. "Ma'am?" she asked. "I need to get a statement from you. If you could come with me?"

"Of course," Emily replied. "Can I just pick up my stuff first?" She gestured to the spilled contents of her purse.

"No problem."

"Emily?" Nick called.

She turned to face him.

"You think we could get a do-over?" he asked.

"I'm afraid to know how you'd top this date." She cocked her head and raised an eyebrow.

"There's only way to find out."

"Cool it, Romeo," said one of the paramedics. "You don't want to get your blood pressure up."

Emily quashed a snicker, but she couldn't stop the instant heat in her face. Was Nick the perfect man for her? Not all of the evidence had been presented, so she decided to grant a continuance.

"This time, I'm picking the restaurant."

Last

And sometimes you can't slam the door fast enough.

Date from Hell

Monica Shaughnessy

JOSIE KRENECK entered Inferno and paused inside the vestibule, jittery with anticipation. On approach, the recently opened eatery resembled an ordinary two-story brick and mortar. But the Virgil brothers, two of the city's hottest restaurateurs, had transformed the interior into a 14th-century church. At some expense, they'd breathed Italian Renaissance into every corner and crevice: marble statues, frescoed ceilings, elaborately tiled floors. Josie didn't know whether to drop to her knees in supplication or speak with the hostess. She decided on the latter and would resort to the former if she couldn't get a table.

"Excuse me," she asked the young woman at check-in, "have you seated an incomplete party?"

The hostess took a leather-bound menu from a stack. "What does your date look like, ma'am?"

"How do you know I'm on a date?"

The girl glanced at Josie's cleavage. It spilled from the top of her tight red dress. "You're not meeting your parents. Not dressed like that."

Josie touched her neckline. Terrific. A college kid with a see-through shirt and a black bra had just confirmed she'd left the house looking desperate. At thirty-five, however, Josie couldn't afford to play hard to get, not when she was halfway down life's path. She'd thrown too many fish back over the years, and the older she got, the less bait she had to offer. Hence, tonight's low-cut, thigh-high, traffic-stopping dress.

"Just tell me what he looks like," the hostess repeated.

"I'm not really sure." Josie shifted from one high-heeled shoe to the other, relieving the pain in her toes. "It's a blind date. So I'm kind of in limbo until I see him." She tightened her fingers around her satin clutch. "But I do know he's got black hair and dark eyes. That's what his profile said."

The hostess's bottom lip quivered. "Him? You're meeting him?" Her gaze shifted to the dining room.

Josie peered into the packed restaurant. Too many customers to know for certain who had drawn the girl's attention. "I guess so," she said with a shrug. "Just show me to his table. I'll take it from there."

The hostess set the menu down and led Josie through the crowded dining area. Patrons' voices bounced off the high ceiling, increasing the volume. A cacophony of emotion, the conversations ranged from shrieks of rage to squeals of ecstasy. She passed one noisy table in particular where a rotund man and his equally stout wife were ripping into a roasted chicken with their bare hands. Josie swallowed her disgust and followed the hostess through a side door marked CONFESSIONAL.

They entered the wood-paneled room and found its lone occupant, a man dressed in black trousers and a black button down shirt, seated at an elaborately carved table for two. He wasn't typically handsome. On the contrary, his fine features could have been classified as boyish, even impish. Yet they gave him a youthful countenance that belied middle age. Black as burned tar, his neatly trimmed hair stood in contrast to his pale skin. The stranger turned and fixed Josie with a powerful stare, communicating on an animalistic level. She was the prey; he was the predator.

The hostess left in a rush, closing the door behind her, shutting out the noise of the main dining room. This left Josie and her date completely alone.

"Handsome Devil?" Josie asked. She used the code name supplied by the dating website, Hot Match.

"None other." The man rose and offered her a seat. Though only a few inches taller than Josie, his presence loomed much larger. "You must be Divine," he said, speaking her code name. His voice was soft and reassuring.

"Yes. That's me." She took the high-backed chair, admiring the gargoyles etched into its surface. "I hope you haven't been waiting long."

"Oh, an eternity," he said. His eyes glittered like the ocean at night, distorted by waves of indeterminate color. Something about this man was different from the others she'd dated, yet eerily the same. "Well, now, Divine, what is your real name? I have a guess, of course, but I want to hear it from your lips." He sat across from her and draped his napkin on his lap.

"Josie Kreneck." The light bulbs flickered overhead. "And you are?"

"I have many names. Lucifer, Azazel, Satariel, Son of Perdition, Destroyer of Souls. Take your pick. One is as pleasing as the next."

Josie rolled her eyes. "Wait. You're telling me that you're—"

"Handsome Devil? That I am." He winked. "And you are simply Divine."

Against her will, her thoughts cleared of all but him. She imagined him biting her neck with his small, even teeth. She shook her head. "There must be some mistake. Hot Match never said anything about setting me up with S-S-"

"Go ahead. You can say it."

"Satan." She bit her fingernail, chipping the red polish. She didn't believe it. Not for a minute. And yet...

"You asked for a bad boy on your profile, didn't you?" He offered a wry smile. "Well, I am the original bad boy."

He poured her a glass of blood red wine. At least she hoped it was wine. She sampled it, letting the tannins coat her tongue, and glanced at the label. Chateauneuf de Pape. The Pope's wine. "I'm not sure I can stay long." She feigned a glance at her watch. "I have plans with friends afterward," she lied.

"You may leave when you truly wish," he said. He lifted the glass in salute and took a long sip.

Josie tried rising from her chair but found her legs too heavy to lift. Did she secretly want to stay? She did find him attractive. In fact, her lust had inexplicably grown these last few minutes. She watched as he opened the menu. His hands clasped the leather cover so gracefully, so tenderly that she found herself wishing he'd touch her with them later, perhaps when they danced. Danced? Not without music. She took another swig of wine. "I can't bring myself to call you Lucifer. How about something close, like Lucas?" she asked.

"Lucas it is," he said, setting the menu aside.

She stared into his eyes, dumbstruck by the color. Emerald green? Not quite. African Ironwood? No, no brown.

"What are we doing tonight?" she asked.

"Whatever you desire. Right now, you want me to touch you. So I will." Lucas reached across the table and stroked her bare arm, searing her skin.

Josie's heart beat faster. The pain was superb. Just what she wanted.

"I may even bite your neck later."

She drew in her breath. "How did you…?"

"I know everything about you, Josie Kreneck. Everything. I have since the day you were born."

The intimacy of his words ignited her body. "If you know everything, then tell me why I find you so fascinating."

"I am an amalgamation of every man you've ever dated. I am neither too tall nor too short, like Cameron, the high school crush that ended badly. My hair is the color of Aaron's, the college boy you fell in love with until you decided you needed a man. If I'm not mistaken, you found several. My skin can only be compared to Daniel's, the man who was set to marry you until you dumped him for Brendan—"

Josie clamped her hand on his black sateen sleeve. "How do you know all this stuff, and why are you torturing me with it?"

"Occupational hazard." He glanced toward the door, and the waitress entered as if he'd summoned her. "Thank Hell you're here. She's famished."

While Lucas ordered for her, Josie's thoughts drifted to her mother and the nickname she'd given Josie in high school. "You're a little sparrow, Josie-bird, flitting from boy to boy," she'd said. Years later, after Josie had jilted her fiancé, her mother's admonishment was more to the point: "You're going to pay for these broken hearts one day, Josie-bird. What comes around goes around." She glanced across the table to her Handsome Devil. Perhaps he'd been telling the truth about himself.

"The kitchen is a little backed up," the waitress said. "We'll do our best." A young girl with a streak of white hair.

"I thought the Virgil brothers held a staff meeting," Lucas said. "I am to get what I want when I want it without argument. Tell the chef if my first course takes longer than ten minutes to arrive, I'll exploit his…unsavory tastes outside the kitchen."

"Yes, sir. What you want, when you want it." She curtseyed. Yes, curtseyed. "You'll get no trouble from us."

As she opened the door to leave, Lucas gave one last order: "Bring a pitcher of ice water for the table. I can't seem to get enough of it."

During the next few minutes, Lucas remained eerily quiet, examining her in silence. This gave Josie the impression, no, the assurance he was reading her mind. Afraid of what else he might uncover, she focused on his eyes, just his eyes. Were they marine blue? Perhaps. Obsidian.

Maybe. By the end of the evening, she would name the color.

The first course, a lovely mozzarella and tomato salad drizzled with olive oil and balsamic vinegar, arrived in eight minutes. She hadn't realized her acute hunger until now. The waitress hadn't brought plates, so Josie decided to eat from the serving platter as delicately as she could with a fork. She searched for a utensil, lifting napkins. "They've forgotten the silverware."

"Eat with your hands," he whispered.

Completely under his spell, Josie did as instructed. She slid her fingers along the plate, grasping a silken moon. She savored the mozzarella, letting the oil run down her chin. She was no better than the gluttons she'd passed in the dining room, the ones who'd been ripping into the chicken.

During the next half hour, course after course arrived: antipasto, lemony calamari, Spaghetti alla Puttanesca, a large bowl of Risotto al Barolo, a sizzling platter of braciole with a mound of herbed vegetables on the side, and finally, two portions of tiramisu—far more than anyone could eat in one sitting, especially with their hands. And yet she ate it all. Every crumb. Every drop. Her appetite disgusted her.

Once the waitress had cleared the dishes, Josie stared at the floor, unable to look her date in the eye. "I'm sorry," she said. "I-I don't know what came over me." She wiped her face, her hands, her arms, soiling the white napkin beyond hope.

"A little gluttony is good for you, my dear."

Josie caught her breath. Gluttony? That was one of the sins, right? She shut her eyes and thought back to her English Lit class at the university. Up to now, the evening had played out like the pages of Dante's Inferno. She glanced at the menu she'd knocked on the floor. INFERNO shone in gold letters on the cover. Lucas chuckled, drawing her attention.

"You're starting to think, aren't you, Josie-bird?" he asked.

Josie-bird? She didn't know it was possible to be terrified and tempted at the same time. Yet she could. not. stand. "Limbo, Lust, Gluttony…" She swallowed. "If I'm not mistaken, Greed is next."

"Consider me your tour guide through the Nine Circles. Tips are optional."

His gaze drew her in again. She couldn't take it anymore. "What color are your eyes?" she finally asked.

"What color do you want them to be?"

"If you're the amalgamation of every man I've ever dated, then I should recognize the color. And I don't."

The corner of his mouth lifted. "Do you like my watch, Josie? It's a Patek Philippe."

She examined the timepiece, admiring the celestial markings on the face. "It's beautiful. How much did it cost?"

"A hundred souls, give or take. In human terms, three hundred grand." He rubbed the watch along her neck. The platinum chilled her skin. "What would you do for an item like this? Would you give me your soul?"

"When Hell freezes over." She sat back and crossed her arms.

"Clever girl." He ran his hand along her thigh, his touch hidden by the tablecloth. "How about your body? Is that for sale?"

She bit her lip.

"A kiss, then. A simple kiss." He leaned across the table. "You can afford that, can't you?"

Josie grasped him by the shirt, pulled him near, and latched her mouth onto his. The act held no sweetness, only the whip-crack of desire. When she broke away and sat down again, the watch encircled her wrist.

"A good purchase," Lucas said. "It suits a whore like you." He wiped a bit of red lipstick from his mouth and licked it from his fingers.

The vulgarity of the statement pushed Josie off-kilter. She didn't know how to respond, or perhaps she couldn't because she knew it was true.

Lucas continued, "Tony couldn't hold you, not with his fumbling backseat attempts. Poor Aaron could barely afford his tuition, but you asked him for that Chanel purse anyway. When he couldn't buy it, you found someone that could. Johnny? Jonathan?" He rubbed his temple. "Forgive me, the names are starting to run together. Then you dumped Daniel, practically at the altar, because his trajectory wasn't sky-high enough. A lowly schoolteacher, you called him. You moved on to Brendan, but that didn't last because he had the audacity to drive a Kia. Each time, you told them...what was it?"

"It's not you, it's me," she mumbled.

"A bit cliché, don't you think?" He settled into his chair. "For months afterward, you swam in a very shallow pool, dipping in and out of men—"

"Shut your mouth! Shut it!" Josie covered her eyes with her hands. "Why are you doing this to me?"

"Surely you read the sign over the door. All sins are laid bare in the confessional." He rose and walked behind her chair. "Are you angry?"

"Yes, very." She wiped her eyes. The watch slid down her arm.

"Splendid. We can move to Circle Six."

"Heresy," she said to herself.

In the background, a melancholy waltz began to play, growing louder and louder until she was certain a group of violinists performed just beyond the wood paneling. Taking her by surprise, Lucas picked her up like a ragdoll and clutched her to his muscular frame. "Shall we dance? Don't deny it. I know you want to," he said.

She melted into his arms, swept away by the force of his touch, as powerful and encompassing as a tsunami. She came up for air and uttered one word: "Yes." It was all she could manage, given tumult in her stomach.

He whisked her around the room, humming all the while. "It's Wagner," he said. "One of my composers. Most people think passion drove his beautiful music." He leaned into her, placing his lips next to her ear. "But it was hatred. He told me so himself."

"Because you put thoughts into his head."

Lucas tipped his head back and laughed. "No, my dear. His thoughts were his own, as are yours. I materialize only when you invite me." His hand pressed the small of her back, making it hard for her to breathe. "I am a little like God in that respect, only not as fickle. I never turn down a request."

"B-but I didn't invite you."

"You didn't?" He batted his long, black lashes. They rimmed eyes of…mercury? Polished iron? Raw steel?

She settled her head on his shoulder. He smelled faintly of campfire. The scent plucked a memory from her head and played it as smoothly as the violins she heard now. She'd invited a few friends over for a Girls' Night In last Saturday, gathering them around her backyard fire pit for cheap wine and drunken confessions. Smoke filled the evening air as she tearfully admitted her fear of growing old. Alone. After downing another half bottle, she'd filled out the dating profile with their help and submitted it. Hot Match contacted her the next day.

"Let me think," Lucas said. He guided them around the table, avoiding the chairs. His lead hand squeezed her fingers. "You asked for a man with black hair, a fair complexion, a well-turned nose, a mischievous bad boy streak, and the power to consume you, heart and soul." He halted their dance and tipped her chin, bringing their lips closer. The music stopped. Her racing heart provided the only rhythm. "Well, Miss Kreneck, here I am."

"No, I-I didn't mean—" He covered her mouth with his, preventing further argument. She resisted his tongue, but it found its way between her lips, burning them like a hot poker. Finding her strength, she turned her head away. "Please let me go. I'll do anything. I'll give you my body. I'll give you my soul. Just let me leave this room!"

"I'm not interested in your soul. I have so many." Lucas sounded like a child who'd grown bored with his toys. He released her and smoothed her hair. "Still, you offered it to me. How easily you turn, heretic."

Josie reared back and slapped him.

"You've dispensed with Circle Seven— Violence—in record time." The angry silhouette of her hand slowly materialized on his cheek. "I'm impressed, little sparrow. Shall I return the favor? It'll be fun." He grinned. "For me."

She dropped to her knees and clasped her hands. "Don't hurt me. I'm begging you."

Lucas stood over her, a look of delight on his face. "You know why you're here, Josie. We've already solved that mystery. But why have you stayed?" He stroked her head. "Hmmm?"

"Because I...I deserve this? For all the hearts I've broken?"

He reached behind his back and produced a whip from thin air. Slowly, he circled her neck with it. "You are a seducer. A panderer. And you must be punished for these sins. Surely you understand this." She didn't argue. Using the whip for leverage, he lifted her to her feet. "Now search a little deeper and find the reason you haven't walked out that door. It's unlocked, Josie."

When she glanced at the door, the raging fire of realization burned through her, leaving her razed and desolate. Her knees buckled. Lucas caught her, letting the whip drop. "I'm here," she said slowly, "because I've chosen to be. Because I want you." She took his face between her hands and gazed one last time into his eyes. Their color had begun to settle, hardening into that of the night sky. Maddeningly, they still they defied description. "Do you want me?" she asked him.

Lucas slipped his hands around her waist and leaned to kiss her. This time, Josie felt, they both craved it. Neither greed nor torture had motivated them. She returned the kiss, submitting to him fully and pressing her body against his. His soft black shirt and wool trousers did little to hide his perfection. She ran her hands along his arms, delighting in the feel of his muscles—hewn of marble, just like the statues in the vestibule. On a whim, she offered her neck to him, which he eagerly took between his teeth. If she was destined to be with Satan, so be it. She could live with that, as long as it meant not growing old alone.

"I'll be right back," he said to her, his voice husky.

"Wait. Where are you going?"

He straightened his shirt and finger combed his hair. "I need to speak to a man about a horse."

"Gotcha," she said. "The bathroom." She gave him a half-hearted smile. "Should I wait here?"

"You can leave if you like. The door will be open." Lucas studied her, his eyes cold. "I've ruined you, Josie. After tonight, you won't want any other man but me. Where else would you go?" He withdrew, leaving the door ajar.

The music had ceased ages ago, but Josie imagined it now as she danced around the room. A few minutes later, she tired of her childish game, and sat down at the table, heady and exhausted from the evening's events. Funny, Lucas had told her she'd be punished for past sins, yet she'd escaped without so much as a whip burn around her neck. She closed her eyes and dreamed of what she would do to Lucas when he returned. Would the table hold them? After a time, she opened her eyes again and checked her Patek Philippe. Nearly thirty minutes had passed. With growing concern, she sat forward to devise her next move. That's when she noticed it: a single white card on the table. She picked it up and read the embossed black letters: IT'S NOT ME, IT'S YOU.

As she crumpled to the floor, she realized the color of his eyes; they were the color of hell.

A Soliloquy of Survival
or First Dates Suck

Ellen Leventhal

THAT ANNOYING ringing! Another solicitor, no doubt. "Unavailable," the caller id says. But not me. I am quite available. Since I kicked him out. Or he left. Whatever it was. A slab of granite to my gut. Should have been a slab of granite to his head. Or another area. Yes, the other area would have been better.

I decide to pick up the phone. What can I lose? "Hello, hello!"

Nothing. Quiet breathing. Someone is there.

The calls come day after day after day. Usually political calls and people selling more insurance. But lately, there have been hang ups. The solicitors are annoying. The hang ups are unsettling. When he was here, he dealt with that. But he's not. And that's that. I promise myself not to pick up anymore.

A knock on the door. It's a delivery. A package from Victoria's Secret. I'm sure it's for the wrong person. I send it back.

I grab the last bottle of Diet Coke from the fridge. Weren't there two last night? I drain the soda and fall into bed. Twisting and turning, I think I hear sounds. But maybe not. I take an Ambien and finally fall asleep. It's after 2:00 am.

I'm woken by noise outside my window. I look at the clock. 7:00 am. I need coffee. I turned the pot on last night, I think. How did it get unplugged? Am I losing my mind? I step into the shower and let the warm water wash over me.

Crash! "Who's there?" Nobody. I need more coffee. And fresh air and a little exercise. So I walk down the three flights of stairs and out into the sunshine.

The sun's rays penetrate the clouds so that they look like a child's drawing. There's a couple across the street looking like they stepped out of a romantic comedy. Flowers and a baguette in a reusable burlap bag. Seriously? At this hour in the morning? Or ever? When did I become a cynic? I'm just practical now. I'm hungry, and I could use that baguette.

I enjoy the balmy weather, but I sense someone or something behind me. Then I hear it. The thumping of footsteps. They get closer, and I walk faster. I remember Mom's advice, and I look for the mace in my purse. Just in case. Click, click,

click. My heels hit the unforgiving cement. Faster and faster. Thump, thump, thump. I can tell the footsteps are those of an approaching man. Now I walk with determination. Head up, eyes forward. The curb! I stumble and twist my ankle. Come on, ankles! Stay with me.

Plop! Down on the ground. I look up. Am I dead? Are angels playing? He looks down at me. The most beautiful face I've ever seen. Dark skin, deep blue eyes, chiseled jawline. "Can I help you, Mona?"

"How do you know my name?"

"Your purse spilled. Your name is all over the sidewalk."

I glance at the items spread out on the ground. I don't see my name. But it must be there. I can't move. Handsome stranger helps me up. We gather the contents of my oversized purse. I'm embarrassed by what's there. Wallet, makeup, mints, tampons, and a small pamphlet titled Finding the Real You. I'm still looking. And the mace.

"Let me walk you home."

"No thanks, I'm fine."

But he makes Dr. McDreamy look like Dr. McDreary. So when he takes my hand, I let him. He walks me home. I can tell that he wants to come in. That's not a good idea. I shouldn't let him in. But what the hell? We both go into the apartment. He goes to the kitchen and gets me ice for my swollen ankle and makes me a cup of tea. How does he know where everything is? We talk. He tells me his name is Atticus. Atticus?

He leaves, I elevate my foot and dive into a book, but I'm too tired to concentrate. And too intrigued with Atticus. Those eyes and the way his mouth turns up. I think about his mouth on mine. I fall into a blissful sleep. I wake up and the smell of coffee draws me into the kitchen. Who made it? My beautiful angel, Atticus? I try to forget about him and go about my day. It bleeds into evening with no delineation. Another in a line of lifeless days. Except for Atticus.

As I move around the apartment I feel vulnerable. I'm not sure why. Someone is watching me. I can't see it, but I feel it. The blinds in the apartment across the street move slightly. Imperceptibly. Someone is there. I'm lonely and bored. Settle down, Mona. It's just your writer's imagination. Save it for the page.

The next morning I'm jarred awake. It's my cell phone. I jump. The handsome stranger is on the other end. My Atticus. I melt. But wonder. Did I give him my cell number? Who cares? He's calling me. I dreamed about him. The old him who left me. And the handsome stranger him who didn't.

I grab the phone. "Sure, Atticus. You can come over later." The minutes turn into hours as they tick away. Waiting. Something niggles at me. Not sure what. I shiver even though it's warm.

I hear the familiar thumping of his feet as he walks up the stairs. I open the door, and I feel my pulse race. He's wonderful, I think. I've been alone too long. "Let's take a walk," he says. We walk the city streets, enjoying the crisp fall air. He puts his arms around me and smiles. "Your ankle healed well," he says.

"Yes, it was just a twist. But, Atticus?"

He answers with a kiss before I finish my question. I never ask. He tells me about his family. I talk about my mother. Her crazy warnings and insane superstitions.

"Ahh, your mother," he says. "I'm sorry for your loss."

I never mentioned she had died. I'm sure of that. How does he know? Clouds begin to cover the sky mirroring my changing mood.

"Having fun?" Atticus asks.

"Yes," I say. Not really knowing.

A seed of doubt. He laughs and grabs my wrist. Not my hand. My wrist. And the seed grows. But he is so handsome. And really quite charming. I remind myself that I am a writer. I imagine. That's my job. I wish away the doubt. He lets go of me, and I relax. We continue to walk. We stop to watch a street artist, and he throws some coins into the waiting violin case. He's a good guy, I think. I forget my reservations and enjoy his company. Time gets away. "I think I better get going now," I say.

"Of course. See you tonight?" he asks. "For a real date?"

"Dinner. I'll cook," I say. His charms make me forget I was ever wary.

"As long as we can go for a drink first. I want to take you to my favorite restaurant."

I go home and fall into my work. The tap of the computer keys feels comforting. The rhythm, the familiarity. And then the door opens. I cock my head. My eyes widen. "You gave me the key before I dropped you off this afternoon," he says.

I take back my key, wondering why I gave it to him. We walk to the restaurant for a drink. I look around. Jimmy Choos, Louboutins, Prada. Out of my league for sure. I wrap my sweater tighter around my JC Penny's dress. We drink wine. I get tipsier and tipsier. "Are you having fun?" he asks.

"Yes, are you?"

"Absolutely," he says. "But the night is young." We go back to my apartment. Why? Double McDreamy is why.

We get to my apartment, and we sit on the couch. Touching. I light candles. "Have another drink, Mona," he says. I hesitate, but really, I want one. Wait! I didn't take my key out. Did I? How did we get in? I spy my key in my open purse. I never took it out. My head is spinning. Was something in that wine? Now I remember that vague uncertainty I had earlier. It's back. Only now it's more pronounced, less vague. I pull away from his touch.

Atticus asks about my brother. "Is he feeling better?" How does he know? My brother has been sick for years. I didn't tell him. I'm certain of it.

I grow uncomfortable and look around the room. What is going on? My eyes land on the coffee table where my dog-eared copy of *To Kill a Mockingbird* stares back at me. Atticus.

I go into the kitchen fully alert now. I bring out dinner. It had been cooking in the crock pot all day. Hot bubbly stew. "Did you finish your work? You spend entirely too much time at the computer," he says.

"You've been watching me," I say.

That smile again. "You're beautiful, but you work too much."

"The keys? How did you do it?" I back away from him and nudge closer to the hot dinner.

"That's easy. Copies of keys can be made anywhere. You should be more careful." He comes closer.

I back away from him. I eye the candles I lit for our romantic dinner.

"I like the yellow negligee you wore last night. But why didn't you wear the one I sent you?"

The strange package from Victoria's Secret. No longer a mystery.

He strides over to me and pushes me against the table. Bowls of hot stew sit precariously near the edge. "And the way you brush your hair, Mona. It's sexy."

How can this be happening? I think. He was so charming. And hot!

He pushes me into the table and holds me tight. He's hurting me, but I'm strong. I arch my body, reaching for a bowl. I need to stretch my arm, but he pulls it back. I hurt, but I still have one free arm. I seize a large bowl filled with hot food. And then I do it. I fling my arm out dumping the whole steaming dinner over his gorgeous head. He can't see, and he backs up. The flame of the candle catches his carefully tailored shirt.

He screams. Some guys can be too hot, I guess. This one was on fire.

Dance
Artemis Greenleaf

WAYNE ALLEN Grady swept an empty beer can off the filthy bedspread so he could sprawl across it. He paid $125 cash every Saturday to rent this room for one more week in what could only charitably be described as a motel. Wayne usually managed to scrape by, begging and doing odd jobs, but the weather had been bad all week. It was Friday afternoon, and he had $12.73.

The management did not extend credit.

He wasn't a con artist at heart, but he preferred grifting to sleeping on the streets in the December rains. Knowing he wouldn't have time to set up a mark and wheedle money in less than twenty-four hours, he would turn to the next best thing. Robbery.

He'd earned bonus money hanging Christmas lights the week before, and he'd charged up his pay-as-you-go cell phone then. It was a good thing, because he was going to need it. Before his friend, Daryl, had gotten busted for theft, he'd shown Wayne how to scrape profiles from one dating site and put them on another. All he had to do was change the name, and make sure he chose sites which were, as Daryl called it, target rich. The weather wasn't likely to get much better anytime soon, so he needed to find a pigeon. But he had to come up with at least $115 before tomorrow afternoon, so he went to the hook-up site first. He had to be careful; most of the ladies there were going to want him to give *them* money, and he needed the cash to flow in the other direction.

He was about to give up and try another site when an ad caught his eye.

> Exotic Dancer Needs You! I'm GiGi, and I dance at a club called Specials. I have been working on some new moves, and I'd love some reviews. I AM NOT A PROSTITUTE - I DON'T WANT YOUR MONEY. Only your opinion. Text me to set up a date!

Wayne sighed. He was skeptical about her not being a prostitute if she was advertising in the hook-up section, but on the other hand, if she was a dancer, she was likely to have cash, and plenty of it. It was worth a try, he decided.

He entered the number into his phone and typed his text. "GiGi- dying to c ur moves. Tonight? Allen"

She texted back almost immediately. "Gr8! Meet me 7:30 @ Taco Shak Gillette &WDallas."

"C U then" he replied.

He wished he had a car. The motel was near the airport, and it would take him at least an hour to make it to midtown by bus. He'd better leave soon to have any hope of getting there by 7:30. Taco Shak sounded cheap, which worked for him.

Better take the gun. He'd found it in a dumpster behind a fast food joint a couple of years ago. Never had any money for bullets – he didn't even know if it worked – but nobody messed with him when he pulled it out.

He tested the tap in the bathroom. The water was turned on today, not something that could be counted on, so he shaved and took a quick shower. No hot water, so it was a very quick shower. Shivering, he put on his other, almost-clean set of clothes. He sprayed himself with cologne he'd gotten from the soup kitchen, or perhaps from the homeless shelter, about this time last year. He put on his threadbare denim jacket more for show than any warmth it might provide and slipped the gun into his pocket.

Wayne was still three blocks away when the text chime on his phone went off. He stopped and looked at it. The time was 7:22, and the text was from GiGi. "Green dress, sitting by the window."

"K almost there."

He hurried along, spurred by the cold gusts of wind. The sky was dull orange, reflecting millions of city lights off of the thick cloud cover, threatening rain.

The movement kept him warm, and by the time Wayne walked up the three rickety steps to Taco Shak's entrance, he was almost sweating. He scanned all the tables near windows. Close to the back was a young woman in a green dress. Wayne's jaw went slack – he couldn't believe his luck. She was gorgeous. Platinum blonde curls bobbed just above her shoulders, and the off-white mug she set on the table came away with a bright red lipstick mark.

Other men stared at her, and Wayne hurried over to claim his territory.

"GiGi?" he asked.

She looked up at him, her bright eyes sparkling. "Yes?"

"I'm W – " he faked a cough. "Allen." He held out his hand for her to shake, awkwardly keeping the palm facing up and his fingers stiff so she couldn't see how filthy his fingernails were.

She giggled slightly as she took his hand. "Nice to meet you. Won't you sit down?"

His coordination failed, and he lurched gracelessly into the booth, facing her across the chipped Formica table. A plastic basket of tortilla chips and two small pots of salsa lay between them.

"I hope you don't mind," she said, "but I was starved, so I went ahead and ordered us some food."

"Um…sure. No problem." He squirmed in his seat, then took a chip.

"It's my treat. You are doing me a huge favor. Thank you so much for coming out."

"Yeah…I didn't know that strip – I mean exotic dancers needed test audiences. I thought if you gals just shake your moneymakers, that's all that's needed." He bit his lip. He sounded like a babbling idiot.

GiGi looked down at the table and played with an empty aspartame packet. "I'm trying to make the International Pole Dancing Championships –"

"Get out of town! They have a contest for that?"

GiGi smiled stiffly.

"Sorry," Wayne said. "I didn't know. Please. Continue on."

She took another sip of coffee. "Anyway, I'm in the regional finals in two weeks. I've been working hard on a new routine. I don't want to do it at the club, because I don't want anybody stealing my moves. But I wanted some audience feedback."

Wayne nodded. He'd been staring at her cleavage instead of paying much attention. Seconds passed in silence.

"Yeah. I'm sure I could do that." He wondered why she needed to advertise. Pretty gal like that could get any hairy-legged man to watch her, easy.

"¡*Comida*!" said the overly enthusiastic waitress. She was an older lady, with wiry grey strands of hair kinking up out of her dull brown ponytail. The woman set down a large tray on the next table and started unloading food in front of them.

"Thank you, Maria," GiGi replied. The server held her eyes for just a moment too long, and Wayne felt a pang of...something. Not fear, not disgust, a vague 'not right' something that made him put his hands in his lap and hunch his shoulders forward, just a little.

He brushed it off when Maria set the sampler platter in front of him. It had a chile relleño, two tacos, a chalupa, and one generous scoop each of refried beans and Spanish rice. Wayne's stomach growled. He couldn't remember the last time he'd had a hot meal. Ramen noodles on the hot plate in his room didn't count. He tried to not to dive in like a hog to slop, but it was hard. He was so hungry, and the food was so good.

This was quite possibly the best first date ever in the history of first dates, he thought. A gorgeous woman, who was planning to dance for him later, had bought him about the best dinner he'd ever eaten. He could get used to this, no doubt about it.

Across the table, GiGi picked daintily at a small green salad.

That must be how she stays so hot.

Now that his belly bulged with warm delectables, he leaned back from the table and let out a long, satisfied sigh. "That was the best Mexican food I ever ate. I'll have to come back to this place."

"I'm glad you liked it," GiGi said. "Maria is a good friend of mine."

"The lady that brought the food? Get out of town. Is she the owner?"

GiGi nodded, then looked at her watch. "My shift starts at ten, so we should probably go back to my place…so I can show you the dance."

"Baby, I'm already there."

GiGi paid the bill with three twenty dollar bills and told the busboy to keep the change. It was a harsh reality check for Wayne, because he'd completely forgotten the whole reason he'd looked for a hook-up for tonight. He was having such a good time that he hated to spoil the evening with a bit of petty larceny. He sighed inwardly. The motel management did not extend credit.

There was no furniture in GiGi's living room. A chrome stripper pole and a folding chair took up the center of it. A few cushions were stacked against the wall.

"Take off your clothes, everything, and sit." GiGi pointed to the chair.

Wayne, sure he knew what was coming, did as he was told. The chair was cold and hard, but he was more than ready for the show. He folded his hands in his lap for some semblance of modesty. The only thing he could think of that would make this date better involved winning lotto tickets.

GiGi turned out the lights. Wayne could hear her moving around in the dark, but couldn't really see her. There was a click, and a single lamp from the track lighting shone on the pole. He didn't see GiGi at first. Then he looked up and saw her hanging upside down like a bat from the top of the apparatus.

Her music started. It was slow, something classical. She spiraled down the pole, her left leg clamped against it, controlling her pace. The music stopped, and so did GiGi. Suddenly, it started up again, fierce, dramatic. The dance changed with the music, and she did several acrobatic stunts involving backflips and gravity-defying rolls up and down the pole. She ran at the pole, then leaped as if she would run straight up it. Instead, she used it as a backstop for a flip with a quarter turn in the air that landed her straddling Wayne's thighs.

She sank into his lap and purred like a kitten. "So, what did you think?"

Her face was not more than six inches from his, and her ample bosom heaved with the exertion of her dance.

At that moment, Wayne couldn't have strung a sentence together if his life depended on it. It wouldn't have helped, anyway.

"Great!" he said. *Would you marry me?*

She laughed, then swooped in and kissed him. Hard, too hard. He reached up to put his hands on her face and push her back. Instead of smooth skin, he felt rough scales. His eyes shot open.

What sat in his lap was not a young, doe-eyed stripper, but something he couldn't explain, even if his eyes told him it was some kind of reptile. He tried to scream, but the creature's tongue filled his mouth, blocking his air.

No one would have suspected that the pile of dust in the folding chair had been human an hour ago. GiGi used her hand to sweep it carefully into a gallon freezer bag. The gun fell out of the jacket pocket when she picked up his clothes, and she set it aside. She emptied her trash into the bag on top of the clothes and tied the open end in a knot. When that was done, she brushed her hair, fixed her lipstick, picked up the remains of her latest would-be paramour and left the apartment. The trash she dropped down the garbage chute, but the gun and the baggie she kept with her.

GiGi tossed the gun into a dumpster behind a fast food joint on her way to Taco Shak. Maria sat at the cash register at the entrance.

"Ahh!" Maria said when GiGi handed her the bag. "My secret ingredient! You know," she told the elderly man who was trying to pay his bill, "my young friend here makes this special spice blend just for me! If we're ever not friends, I may as well shut my kitchen."

GiGi winked at the old man and left.

Forever

Once in a great while, a first date is the first glimpse of forever.

Cassie

Artemis Greenleaf

"WHAT DO you mean you didn't get the cancelation insurance?" I asked. "How could you not get cancelation insurance for an event in September? How long have you lived in Houston?"

"It was expensive, Marti. Mom and Dad are already giving us a house," Emily replied.

"That Mr. Petras left them when he died. It was free. They were glad to give it to you so they could stop paying taxes on it."

My sister sighed. "The storm in the Gulf is TD 11 – a tropical depression. That doesn't necessarily mean it will turn into a hurricane."

"It doesn't have to. Remember all that crazy flooding with Tropical Storm Allison? Besides, Channel 2 predicts it will be a hurricane by tomorrow night." I flicked through the channels. "So does Channel 11. And Channel 13."

Emily shrugged. "On the plus side, we didn't choose the beach wedding, like we'd originally talked about doing."

I laughed, then fluffed up my hair. "Yeah, the Bahamas would have been bad this weekend. Good thing you and Nick decided to go hiking in Yellowstone for your honeymoon instead." I fixed my lipstick. "You ready to go celebrate your last night as a single woman?"

Heavy clouds glowered over the outdoor wedding chapel. Gusts of wind tugged at the satin bows on the aisle-side chairs, but so far, there wasn't any rain. No one would know that to look at Mom – her mascara ran down her face like she'd just come out of the swimming pool. *Glad we did pictures earlier.*

The music started.

Mom handed Emily her bouquet. "Love you, baby."

"Love you too, Mom."

Dad waited in the staging area to escort her down the aisle to the front row of seats. I thought he managed very well, given the uneven ground. He came back along the outside of the chairs so he could walk with Emily when the time came. But now, it was my turn. I peeked at Nick, standing at the front of the chapel and thought he looked very handsome in his white tux. But quite not as handsome as my escort, Ryan. I liked that he was tall enough for me to wear heels and still be shorter than him. Which is rare, because I'm 5'9". Of course, this is one of the reasons Emily paired us up to walk down the aisle. He smelled just as nice today as he had when we'd practiced walking down the aisle and lining up at the rehearsal last week. I would have talked to him longer at the rehearsal dinner, but he had to go to work. He told me he normally worked day shift, but his schedule was a little crazy because he rearranged it so he could take the entire weekend off for the wedding. Like Nick, he was a cop, and they often ran calls together. I was surprised I hadn't seen him at some point during one of my shifts in the ER. Trauma nurses meet a lot of police officers.

Ryan smiled at me when he offered his arm, and I hoped that I had on enough makeup to mute the blush I felt scorching my cheeks. Made it hard to feign aloofness.

The ceremony was short and sweet. No one fainted, fumbled their words, or tripped over their long skirts. Nick and Emily had planned to light a unity candle, but the wind wouldn't cooperate, so they opted to do it at the reception. Fortunately, Tranquil Pines Ranch, the wedding venue, had an indoor option for the reception, because large raindrops started to splatter on the wedding guests during the 'you may now kiss the bride' part. High heels and taffeta notwithstanding, the wedding party was the first to flee into the reception hall. Actually, it was the venue owner's tiny 1950's ranch-style house. Worst case scenario – the weather could have forced Emily to have had the ceremony in there, too, if she'd didn't mind getting married in a stranger's kitchen.

I stopped to help my dad because his prosthetic leg slowed him down. Mom pulled out her umbrella to cover Dad and me, but she wasn't quite tall enough and kept jabbing me in the face with the ends of the ribs. Ryan took the umbrella from her and sent her on into the reception hall. Emily and Nick stopped too, but he waved them on. Fortunately, the rain didn't begin in earnest until after we all got inside, and Ryan wasn't too wet.

"Thanks," I said, smiling at him.

"My pleasure."

He held my eyes a little too long. Emily tapped on a glass, shattering the gaze. "I have an announcement. TD 11 is now a tropical storm, and we're starting to see some of the outer rain bands. So we're going to get all the fun stuff done so that anybody who wants to leave early has a chance to dance. We're going to do the unity candle, do the first dance, and then cut the cake."

The dance floor was the screened-in porch, but gusty winds drove sheets of rain through the mesh, soaking even the dancers who stayed in the half closest to the house. Most of the guests had already left by the time Emily tossed the bouquet at me, her two college roommates, and Mom's widowed elderly neighbor, Mrs. Paddington. *Good grab, Mrs. P.!* Emily and Nick left as soon as the flowers were caught – they were going to try to catch an earlier flight before the really bad weather moved in.

"Hey, Marti?" Ryan asked. "I'm going to change out of this monkey suit and go grab a bite. Would you like to come?"

"Sure. Where do you want to go?"

"How about Sweet Tomatoes on I-10?" he replied.

"Sounds good. I'll change into my normal clothes, too. Meet you back out here, then I'll follow you?" The butterflies were flapping so hard in my stomach that I wasn't sure I'd be able to eat anything.

"Okay. See you in a minute."

When we went out to our cars, the rain had let up, and there was even a glimmer of sun. But it was sandwiched between thick black clouds, so I doubted it would last. But then again, sometimes completely unexpected things happened with tropical storms and hurricanes. Not unlike dinner dates.

Ryan and I both reached for the door handle at the same time, and our fingers brushed together. *Were his hands always this warm?*

The usually packed restaurant was nearly empty, and I briefly wondered if it might be better to skip dinner and get home. But I glanced at Ryan and decided against the sensible option.

The skies stayed clear while we made our way through the salad line and got bowls of soup. The weather app chimed on my phone. TD 11 was now a Category 2 hurricane, steaming towards Corpus Christi. If it stayed on track, we'd be on the dirty side of the storm. As my dad had explained it to me, the storms rotate counter-clockwise, so the most rain is on the right half – it's either precipitated out or spun off into smaller squall lines by the time the winds swing back around to the left side.

It wasn't long after that rain began to bucket down, cutting visibility to zero. The world outside could end, and we'd wouldn't know it.

"Leave it to Emily to pick a hurricane weekend to get married," I said.

"Rain on your wedding day is supposed to be lucky," Ryan replied.

"Is it?" I looked up into his eyes. They were very dark brown, almost black.

He looked back at me with a slight smile on his face. "It's a sign of fertility."

I quickly looked down and dunked my bread in my country vegetable soup. "You don't know my sister very well. I think Nick'll be lucky if he gets one kid." I half smiled. "Although I'm sure it won't be from lack of trying." *OMG. Did I really just say that? It came out completely different from what I meant.* I dug into my salad.

Ryan laughed. "I'm sure you're right."

"I meant lack of trying to persuade her."

"I see."

"So…how about those Rockets?"

"Basketball season hasn't started yet."

Of course it hasn't. "Well, didn't they just sign some expensive new guy?"

He was clearly amused at my athletic franchise ineptitude. "Most teams do that every year."

I took a sip of tea. "Yeah," I confessed. "I don't really follow sports. But it usually starts guys talking. Once they get going, they don't notice that I haven't said much, and I win bonus points for bringing up sports." *Was that too much information?*

"We're pretty predictable."

I stretched out my legs and kicked his ankle.

I looked up at him. There was a bemused smile on his face.

"I am so sorry," I said, heat rising to my cheeks. I pulled my feet back under my chair.

"It's alright," he replied.

From the look on his face, I was pretty sure that he thought I'd done it on purpose. He was wrong about that, though. I hadn't intended to *kick* him.

Lightning flashed, and a peal of thunder shook the building. I jumped, nearly falling out of my chair. Ryan stood up to reach across the table and steady me. His fingers grazed my collarbone, and a hot shiver of pleasure vibrated down my spine.

The power went out, and the emergency lights above the exits came on. There was a collective groan from the diners, especially the handful who were in line to pay.

Seconds passed. No power. "Must have hit the transformer," Ryan said. He got out his cell phone and activated the flashlight app. Cell phone lights dotted the restaurant – it was almost like a candlelight dinner. "I'm just going to take a look around outside. You stay here, okay?"

I shrugged, happy enough not to be going out into the rain, but not wanting to be left behind, either. *That's me – seething mass of contradictions, at your service.* I followed him to the glass door and looked around. Everything in the strip center across the street was also dark.

I watched Ryan walk around under the overhang of the restaurant, mostly out of the driving rain. He sent a text and came back inside. I followed him to our table.

"There's a flash flood warning. And a river flood warning, and you know White Oak Bayou always floods – we're just down the road from that." He raised his glass and took a big drink of iced tea. "I think we ought to finish here and go home. Why don't you let me drive you? I've got a truck, and you've got a little car – if water comes up fast, I've got more clearance, and the truck's a lot heavier."

"That sounds like a great idea, except that I need my car to get to work tomorrow. With this storm, I may even have to go in tonight." I picked at the blueberry muffin on my plate.

Ryan nodded. " I'll follow you, then. If you're ready, why don't we go now? "

"Just let me finish my tea." I stood up and took a deep draft through the straw. "Let's go."

Once I got in the car, I backtracked down surface roads to get to one that went under the freeway, and I didn't have to make a U-turn. Unfortunately for me, the intersection had flooded, and water was well up over the curb. I would have to get on the feeder and turn around anyway. The rain had slacked off some but hadn't stopped. Strong wind gusts pushed against my car and made the steering difficult. I checked my rear view mirror. I still had my escort. I felt myself grinning like an idiot when I saw his reflection in the glass.

The break in the storm was short lived. Strong winds drove the rain horizontally, making handling the car tricky. I may as well have been driving through a car wash, the downpour was so heavy. I turned the windshield wipers on high, but the rain bucketed down on the glass as fast as they could clear it. Water covered the left lanes of the feeder, but the right lane was passable. I hoped, anyway – I could barely see it. It wouldn't be clear for long. I drove as fast as I dared, screaming down the road at 16 MPH. I was glad to get to the overpass, out of the flood, although streams of rainwater flowed down the arch of the bridge. We were in the part of town where I-10 is one enormous concrete bayou. I couldn't see far enough down to tell if it was filling up with water, but my guess was that it was. Another lightning bolt cracked across the sky, and the whiplash of thunder shook my car.

Something thudded into my windshield. I jumped and hit the brakes, too hard, and started to skid. My car slid sideways as a large white bird flopped helplessly on my hood. I took my foot off the gas and tried to steer in the direction of the skid. The only problem with that was that I was now crossways on the overpass. The car bumped the curb and stopped before it crashed through the guardrail. *Somebody must be looking out for me because I don't see how that little curb stopped the car.* The bird – an egret – flapped one wing while the other dangled limply. The fierce wind nearly bowled the poor thing over. He would have to go to the wildlife rehabbers as soon as the storm passed. I grabbed the top from my spare pair of scrubs and got out of the car. The shirt wasn't nearly big enough to cover the long-necked, long-legged bird. Rain battered my face and pushed my hair down into my eyes, making a tough rescue that much harder.

"Dude, where have you been?" I asked the bird when I noticed a red sequin stuck to one of its feet. I found that I was humming 'Summertime,' from *Porgy and Bess*, one of my mom's favorite songs. How that came to be in my head, I'll never know. Mystery earworms happen to everybody sometimes, I guess.

"Are you okay? What are you doing?" Ryan shouted against the wind as he pulled up in his truck and rolled down the window a couple of inches. He must have seen me sliding around like the *Ice Capades* on top of the bridge.

"Bird hit my windshield. Think its wing is broken." I shouted back, pointing to the flapping egret.

A moment later, I heard Ryan's door slam. He had a jacket in his hands. Together, we wrangled the injured bird into his truck. It was a double cab, and he didn't have a cardboard box, so we put the bird in the back seat. The egret wasn't happy with this arrangement, and it squawked and flapped for several minutes before settling down. I sat in the front seat with Ryan and shivered. He started up the truck and turned on the heat. Gale force winds will chill you right down when you're soaking wet.

"I'm not sure anybody I know would run out into a hurricane to help an injured bird."

"Except for me." I rubbed my arms, trying to warm them.

He nodded. "Except for you." He leaned over and opened the glove box. After a moment of searching, he pulled out a small silver packet. "We can't have you shivering, now can we?"

I shook my head.

He opened the packet and pulled out a silver thermal emergency blanket and wrapped it around my shoulders. Then he moved over and sat very close. "For warmth," he said.

"Of course."

The music on the radio stopped and emergency claxon screeched, causing the egret to squawk and flap a few times. "The National Weather Service in League City has issued a flash flood warning until 7:00 PM Monday for the following counties: Brazoria, Chambers, Harris, Galveston, Liberty. Do not attempt to drive into

Page ❤ 121

high water. Hurricane Cassie is still hours away from landfall and continues to strengthen and is likely to be a Category 3 or higher by the time it makes landfall late this evening. Current projections have the storm coming ashore just east of Corpus Christi. Additionally, the Weather Service has issued a tornado watch for the entire listening area until 8:00 PM on Monday." The music returned.

"Looks like we might be here a while," Ryan whispered in my ear.

"Looks that way," I replied, snuggling closer.

In the Mood

Mandy Broughton

JAZZY BRASS blared in the darkened room as saxophones and percussion beat out a light rhythm from Glen Miller's "In the Mood." Luella Trelotte tapped a toe in appreciation. The science teacher watched those dancing, or rather loosely labeled as dancing, as they squeezed their dates too tight, invaded each other's space, and swayed much too slowly to match the music. She sighed. Students no longer learned the art of foxtrot, swing, or cha-cha. Posture and poise had no place in a high school gym these days.

The doors swung open revealing a medium-height, balding man. Luella jumped in surprise at the newcomer, but those on the dance floor continued dancing. Obviously, they were oblivious to the entrance of the surprise guest. The all-business, no-frills principal had never attended a school dance. Luella's heart beat faster as she watched him make his way to the refreshment table. Their brief encounters at school were exciting. She looked forward to Mondays when she would run into Principal Gerald Reading in the hallway or at lunch.

Luella screwed up her courage. She would join him at the punch table but vowed to avoid the subject of the latest scandal. She patted her hair and wished for the hundredth time that, for once, it would have cooperated with her. She'd tried—and failed—for a classic 1920s updo with a single large curl and wave. Instead, it looked as if her normally straight dishwater blonde hair had been frizzled with a finger to the electrical socket.

Principal Reading looked up as she crossed the room. He graced her with a rare smile. She straightened her shoulders, and her step was a little lighter. She smiled back.

"Good evening, Ms. Trelotte," he said. His suit was worn but was neat and well cared for. It was easily twenty years old, but fit as if he'd just left the department store this morning. "Care for a punch?" He held out a plastic cup half-filled with a pink drink and frothy top. "Sherbet and Sprite, if my taste buds do not deceive me." His hand shook slightly, causing some liquid to slosh. Luella frowned. He quickly grabbed a napkin and dabbed the sides of the cup.

"Thank you, Mr. Reading." Luella accepted the cup and sipped. She sucked her stomach in, trying to make her classic red wrap-around dress fit properly. Instead, like her hair, the dress had a mind of its own. It bunched up in all the wrong places. "The Big Band Theme is more popular than I thought it would be," she said releasing her breath. The dress wouldn't cooperate. She might as well be comfortable. "The dance floor is packed."

The principal smoothed his blue tie, making sure it stayed behind the one button of his double-button down suit jacket. Flashy ties on men in their fifties had no place in a high school gym either. "Catchy music," he said smoothing his tie again. Luella felt it had almost become a nervous tic for him.

She nodded. "I like it. It almost makes me forget what a rough year it's been." All previous vows to avoid the subject were thrown out the window. She wanted to know, and Mr. Reading had always been willing to volunteer information, no matter how distasteful. "Have you started interviewing for a new band director yet?" She licked her lips. "Since we're in such a small town, I know it takes time to attract quality teachers," she added hastily.

"Ms. Trelotte, I may not have the privilege much longer to search for quality replacements," he confessed. He stared as the D.J. keyed up the next piece. "Moonlight Serenade." She watched, surprised again, as the principal swayed slightly to the music before stopping himself. "I may be relieved of my duties as principal."

Luella choked on her drink. She dabbed her neck with a napkin, cleaning up the spill. She'd forgotten to wear a necklace, again, and the plunging neckline, safety-pinned for modesty, didn't suffer from the spilled libations. Exposed cleavage was for those teachers who'd run off with married men. "Superintendent Georges--"

"Blames me," Gerald finished. He smiled a small ironic grin. "But let's not talk shop tonight. Ms. Trelotte, you look lovely."

Luella flushed as red as her dress. "I'm a disaster." She touched her hair. "The kids must think I shocked myself with this afternoon's experiment. And that diet I've been one, well, I have only fifteen pounds to go from the ten I originally wanted to lose."

Gerald grabbed her free hand, the one not clutching a half-empty punch glass. "You look lovely," he insisted. His eyes roved over her failed fashion attempt. "I'd much rather have a competent science teacher than a super-model." He paused, must have realized what he said, then flushed. "I'm sorry. That came out wrong, I meant--"

"It's okay," Luella said. She squeezed his hand before dropping it. She'd never known him to grab her hand, or any other teacher's hand, for that matter. "I know what you meant, especially with all that's gone on this year." She smiled. "And I'd rather be known for competency, anyway."

Gerald smiled but said nothing. Luella thought he had pretty teeth. She wished he were able to smile more. As she tried to think of something else to say, he leaned closer, his breath smelling sweet from the sherbet and Sprite. "I thought your presentation to the students on STEM careers was particularly rousing."

Shocked, Luella stood up straight. "I, um, thank you," she finished lamely.

The D.J. queued up another piece. A heavy brass three-four time rhythm came into being.

"'The Last Waltz,'" Gerald said. "I love this piece."

Mr. Reading wasn't acting like himself; attending a school dance, squeezing her hand. It was unheard of from her, normally very predictable, principal. She sucked in a deep breath. She would not be detoured. "Superintendent Georges has no right to blame you. All you've ever done is support learning. You can't be blamed for what others choose to do in secret." She bit her lip nervously, wondering if she should continue. She tread on unsteady footing but plunged ahead anyway. "It's unfortunate about the scandal, for the band director, Mr. Fielding, to have an affair with Mrs.--"

Gerald turned to her and held out his hand. "Shall we dance, Ms. Trelotte?"

"I..." Luella's voice failed her. The punch didn't taste spiked. Besides, Mr. Reading would never allow alcohol on his campus. He cared for the students on and off campus entirely too much. Luella didn't know how to explain his current mood. "Do you know how to waltz?" she asked.

"I do," Gerald said. He looked as if he were about to say more but declined. Instead, he asked, "Do you?"

Luella nodded. "But what about decorum?"

"We have chaperones," he said nodding toward a cluster of teachers in the corner. Gerald continued, "Although I'm concerned that they're playing 'The Last Waltz' far too early in the evening. Shouldn't it be last?" Luella giggled despite herself. The principal took her hand and led her to the dance floor. The crowd of students parted. Gerald clasped one hand to Luella's hip and led her around the dance floor. As they circled, students fell back and shouted comments.

"Ms. Trelotte, where did you learn to dance?" a male student yelled.

"Simple physics," Luella answered as Gerald lifted his hand, and she spun underneath.

"Mr. Reading, you need to be on *Dancing with the Stars*," a female student shouted.

"I turned them down," he said good-naturedly. "I told them I had students to discipline and dreams to crush. Keeping you all downtrodden and helpless is full-time work." The students laughed. Despite his firm and cool exterior, Principal Reading was a popular man.

"The school needs you," Luella whispered. "Especially now. The students know you care about them." Luella stared into his brown eyes.

"And the teachers?" he asked his voice husky.

Luella's heart skipped a beat. She tripped over her feet and caught herself before falling. "We know you care for us, too," she squeaked.

Gerald nodded and brought her into another twirl as if she had never stumbled. The music ended, and they clapped. The students cheered.

"That was fun." Luella laughed, out of breath. "I haven't done that in ages."

"Physics aside, where did you learn to dance?" Gerald asked.

"I'm a terrible athlete so when I was growing up my parents put me in dance for off-campus physical education." Luella sighed. "I've never been able to use it. Men tend not to ask me to dance that often," she said. "Or ever." Luella pushed the past away. She exhaled heavily. "What about you?" she asked. "Where did you learn to dance?"

A faraway look came over Gerald. He sucked in a deep breath and closed his eyes. Luella felt she had tread on something sacred. "I—thank you for the dance." She pulled away.

The D.J. popped in another jazzy, swinging big band song. Gerald refused to let go of her hand. He blew air through his lips slowly. She felt his hand relax. He opened his eyes. A mischievous glint blossomed. "How's your foxtrot?"

"Two requests in one night?" She fanned herself. "This is unknown territory." She patted her frizzy hair again. "I can foxtrot, but what about the students?" All at once, as if they heard her objections, the students began chanting and clapped in beat, "Dance, dance, dance."

Luella's shoulders sagged in defeat. She closed her eyes, straightened her posture, and turned into a foxtrot champion. "Let's show them who the real *Dancing with the Stars* are," she said recklessly.

Feet flew as Gerald led her around the floor. Step, step, step. Twist, twirl, follow his lead. Students cheered, clapped, and a few even, wolf whistled. Heat rose to her neck and not from just the jaunty fast-paced piece. She enjoyed the feel of the heat from Gerald's hand on her hip. Just when she thought she would collapse, the song ended. Luella panted as Gerald bowed to her, thanking her for the dance. His phone vibrated, he pulled it out and excused himself while Luella stayed on the dance floor.

"Ms. Trelotte, does Otis need to carry you to a chair?" Ed Darem, the quarterback of the River End football team, asked.

Otis, a three hundred pound, six-foot-three-inch sophomore held out his arms. "I help my Mama when her hip starts paining her."

"I'm fine, boys," she said, clutching her side. "I'm just not used to exerting myself outside the lab."

"Practice, practice, practice," Ed said, pitching his voice higher, trying to mimic his teacher. "Science isn't about getting it perfect when you experiment. It's about doing and doing again. Repeatedly."

Luella laughed, despite the stitch in her side. "I'm glad you listen in class."

"We may not make the grades," Otis grunted. "But we always listen."

"Otis thinks you're the greatest teacher, ever," Ed said in a conspiratorial whisper. "He threatens the team with bodily injury if they don't pay attention in physics."

"Thank you, Otis, for the support," Luella said. She found a chair and sat. "But I don't want you to get in trouble." Otis just grinned. Trouble and Otis were best buddies.

Ed ducked his head. "Speaking of trouble, is it true Mr. Reading is getting sacked?" Ed's forehead wrinkled.

"Where did you hear that?" Luella demanded.

"It's a small town, Ms. Trelotte," Otis said. "And Mr. Darem's on the board. Ever since Mr. Fielding ran off with Superintendent George's wife--"

"Please." Luella held up a hand. "I don't want to discuss it further."

"Mr. Reading is a good principal," Otis said.

"It's not fair to punish him," Ed added. "He wouldn't punish us unfairly."

"Thank you, boys," Luella said firmly this time. "But it's out of our hands."

The boys nodded and Otis brought her another punch. She gulped it greedily.

"You're a good teacher. And you look pretty when you smile," Otis told her. Luella's eyes widened, she didn't want another scandal on her hands. She would straighten the football player out as gently as she could. She opened her mouth but stopped. Otis watched Mr. Reading re-enter the gym. "You deserve to be happy," he said. "So does Mr. Reading." Otis shuffled off to join his friends. Luella placed her drink to the side. Sage advice came in the oddest of places.

Gerald Reading pulled up a chair and joined Luella at the corner of the dance floor. More trumpets and trombones blasted from the speakers. The noise and crowd of students gave them an oddly private conversation.

"Bad news?" she asked watching his face.

"The school board is holding an emergency meeting on Monday. My presence has been requested for the second hour of the meeting."

"I'm sorry--" Luella started but Gerald held up a hand.

"I have no control over teachers who conduct themselves inappropriately," he said. "But that doesn't matter. We've had a scandal. Despite my best attempts to weed out the chaff, some got through."

"Finding good teachers is hard," Luella said.

"Especially for this small town," Gerald agreed. "We were bound to get in trouble by taking everyone who applied."

"You didn't--"

"I refused to hire the band director but the board overruled me."

Luella digested that. Mr. Reading had not wanted to hire the band director, but the board hired him instead. And now Gerald was blamed for the board's mistake.

"I don't feel quite like myself," Gerald confessed. "I feel dangerous."

Luella's eyes widened. "It'll be okay. Please don't hurt yourself. The students and I still love you." She placed her hands over his.

Gerald laughed and patted her hand. "No, no, no. I would never hurt myself or anyone else, for that matter. I'm tickled at your concern, though." He paused, evidently deep in thought. Luella tried to figure out a way to extricate her hands but she found she liked the coarse feel of his fingers.

"Superintendent Georges is a vindictive man," Gerald said. "He's lashing out, and I regret that I'm the one in his sights." Gerald threaded his fingers through hers. "I feel reckless tonight. I feel like being the man they think I am."

"What do you mean?" Luella leaned in, curious. She enjoyed talking with him. He was knowledgeable, learned, and very compassionate.

Superintendent Georges, on the other hand, was loud, brash, and unconcerned with anyone except himself. Luella avoided him like potassium and water.

"Dangerous." Gerald loosened his tie but clasped her hand again before she could pull it away. "I've kept proper decorum in this school for years. All the work. But none of that matters to Georges. And now..." his voice trailed off. "The dancing," he said. His lip upturned slightly, giving him a lopsided smile. "My wife and I took dance lessons for years."

Luella pulled her hands-free. He never, *never*, talked about his wife. She knew he kept her photograph on his desk, but never spoke about her. Even his secretary would tear up when asked about the late Mrs. Reading.

"She loved to dance. And I loved her," he said. "So I learned to dance."

"I'm sorry," Luella said, knowing it was completely inadequate.

"It's been ten years." He steepled his fingers, his eyes never looking up. "And I miss her still. But tonight, with the thought of losing my job. Everything I've worked for, it makes me wonder."

"Wonder what?" Luella asked.

"Do you remember your interview? Last year?"

Luella blushed. "It was a terrible interview. I accidentally broke your lamp in my exuberance about explaining my latest experiment."

"And you took it home and fixed it."

"Well, yes. Being rather clumsy, I have gotten good at fixing things."

Gerald raised his head. His eyes caught her. Her heart stopped at the look he gave her.

"I fell in love with you, Ms. Trelotte. Clumsy. More concerned about learning versus your appearance. A desire to give students a passion for science. You radiated heat. Warmth. Excitement." He moistened his lips. "I felt like I had woken up after ten years of sleep after meeting you."

Luella sat there. She couldn't have heard him correctly. Her ears had stopped working, and she must have been imagining the entire conversation. Blood rushed to her head and caused a roar in her ears. Gerald tapped her knee, softly and affectionately. His face showed no expression, but his brown eyes said it all. Luella's heart pounded in her chest. Dumpy, science-nerd Luella, whom men ignored unless they needed help with a project or an answer to a difficult question. A man had professed his love for her. And that he even liked to be around her.

She wanted to say she loved him back. That she looked forward to their little meetings in the hallway. She enjoyed his thoughts and ideas about where the science department should go in the future. Leading and teaching kids to be lovers of science. But instead, she told him, breathlessly, "The school can't take another scandal."

"No," Gerald agreed. "It is improper for a principal to date one of his teachers. And I will never bring disgrace to the school."

"So why..."

Gerald sighed. "Life is short. Too short. I've given my all to the students," he said. "I'd like to continue, but after Monday, I may not be able to."

"So..."

"I wanted to tell you," Gerald said simply. "You're a remarkable woman, and one should always be truthful with remarkable women." Luella sat in stunned silence. Gerald cocked his head to the side. "'Sunrise Serenade.' Another great piece. Shall we dance again?"

Luella nodded robotically. She didn't trust herself to answer. She felt ashamed that she briefly considered forgetting decorum and didn't care if she brought more scandal to the school. But Gerald was correct. The students were more important than her immediate happiness. She followed Gerald's lead across the dance floor. The students must have sensed something because they left the couple alone this time. The medium tempo music kicked Luella's brain back into gear. She was a scientist. She knew how to solve problems.

"It's a small town," Luella said.

"Indeed," Gerald said.

"We can't date," she explained.

"No," he agreed.

"If you are fired..."

"I would leave town immediately. I wouldn't ask you to leave with me. The students need you." He brushed a frizzy lock off her face. "I would never be that selfish. They still need to learn. And you are the best science teacher by far. And if we did date after my firing, it would still cause a scandal. People would make up rumors."

"You may not be fired," she said. "Just disciplined."

Gerald nodded.

Luella felt the rhythm of the music in her bones. She hadn't danced in years, but dancing with Gerald was easy. It was as if she belonged there. Thirty years were nothing to the muscle memory in her feet.

"Since it's a small town," Luella said, "the board does have exceptions."

"Not to dating." Gerald narrowed his eyes as if to question her line of thought.

"They allow people in the same school," she coughed not knowing if she could get it out. Gerald had called her remarkable. She would be remarkable if only, for an evening. "They allow husbands and wives to work in the same school, like a principal and a teacher."

Gerald stopped dancing and gaped at her. Luella smiled coyly. For the first time this evening, she felt she had jarred him instead of the other way around.

"A principal can be married to one of his teachers." Luella tugged at her partner, encouraging him to dance again. Luella was feeling rather dangerous herself. "They have to allow it, because that's how it used to be, ages ago." She laughed. "This is a small town, remember?"

Gerald started forward again and Luella resumed her backward dancing. He didn't say anything. She continued smiling.

"We'll need to be back by Monday," Gerald finally said.

Luella laughed. "We could catch a red-eye to Vegas, maybe one of the teachers can drive us to the airport."

"I may lose my job but, hey, life is short. Last minute ticket to Las Vegas shouldn't stop us." He grinned back at her. "Sure, let's do it."

"Agreed," Luella said. She allowed him to move in closer to her personal space.

The song ended. They clapped politely and headed to their spot by the punch bowl. "It's a fun joke," Luella finally said. "It's great to imagine someone wanting me." She stopped. "No, desiring me. But I'm used to being the butt of everyone's jokes. And I respect you greatly so if you don't mind, we can go back to reality--"

"Mr. Austin. STEPHEN!" Gerald bellowed across the gym. Students, teachers, and parents stopped and stared. Even the D.J. lowered the volume on the music. "I have a favor to ask."

The history teacher answered. "Sure, Mr. Reading. I'd be happy to help."

Aware that everyone was watching them, Gerald spoke even louder. "I need a ride to the airport tonight."

Luella clutched Gerald's hand. "Are you crazy?" she hissed.

"Going into the city, no problem," Mr. Austin said. "I'd be happy to drop you off."

Gerald gave Luella's hand a quick squeeze before letting go. He rubbed his hands together. She realized bold Mr. Reading was nervous. She felt sick to her stomach. She was never bold. Unsure and unsteady were her companions. "What is happening?" she whispered.

"I may have a passenger with me. Wait, let me ask her," he said. Gerald Reading glanced at Luella Trelotte. She trembled.

Smiling, Gerald dropped to one knee. Luella gasped. The gym spun around her.

"Ms. Trelotte," he said taking her hands in his, "will you marry me?"

The gym hushed. Stars danced before Luella's eyes. She looked at Gerald on one knee, took a deep breath, and let it out slowly.

"Okay," she said.

The gym exploded in noise. Kids cheered. Boys whacked their principal on the back. Girls hugged Ms. Trelotte. Teachers and parents twittered about, hugging and crying each other and Luella.

"I may be unemployed by Tuesday, Ms. Trelotte," Gerald whispered in her ear.

Luella smiled. "That's okay. We'll survive. But you can call me Luella now."

"Oh, not yet," Gerald told her with humor in his eyes. "I am a stickler for decorum. It's Ms. Trelotte until after the ceremony."

"Certainly, Mr. Reading," she agreed.

"Let's go get married," he whispered to her.

She squeezed his hand. "Okay."

Famine's Daughter
Artemis Greenleaf

May 14, 1184
Annual Trade Summit

KEIKO SAT at a table on the wide balcony, watching the seabirds skimming over the surf in search of fish, and wishing she was somewhere else. If only she could go fly along the beach, just like the gulls.

"Ambassador Ogoncho?"

She turned to see one of the European representatives, Tristan Rathmore, standing at her table. He was tall, and the sea breeze played with his sandy hair. "Yes?" Keiko asked, folding her fan while she spoke.

"I'm terribly sorry to bother you – I know the summit is finished for the day – but do you have a moment to discuss cinnabar exports?" he asked in perfect Japanese.

Keiko glanced to the double doors that led to the interior dining rooms. "Of course. Please sit down," she replied in English.

"Thank you."

Her multi-layered *jūnihitoe* was not well-suited to the tropics, and her luxurious ankle length hair added to her discomfort. She had defied social convention and braided it to get it off the back of her neck. Keiko hoped he would not be offended by her lack of decorum.

A servant in a white linen tunic was at the table before Tristan finished straightening his chair. "Beverage, milord?"

"Saké, please."

"Yes, milord."

"Saké is not a drink for everyone," Keiko said.

"My business sometimes takes me to Kyoto. I've rather developed a taste for it."

She was amused but tried not to show it. Instead, she picked a piece of lint off her silk *jūnihitoe*. "What was your question about the cinnabar?"

"Cinnabar?" he asked. "Ah, yes. The cinnabar exports. My agents in Kyoto tell me that there is a troublesome clan, the Minamoto, causing some instability in the provinces. Our local Council relies heavily on the income from selling cinnabar to area alchemists. I realize, of course, that you cannot spend all of your time supervising the matters of these men." Tristan smiled.

Keiko nodded but kept her face unreadable. *He is handsome, even if he is Gaikokujin, a foreigner.* "Yes, Clan Taira and Clan Minamoto joined together to defeat Clan Fujiwara, but they had a falling out. Now they strive against each other. *Daimyo* – warlords – can be most temperamental."

"Yes, I suppose they can. There has also been much unrest amongst the royals in England of late. Richard and Henry the Younger battle most grievously against their father, King Henry."

Keiko nodded politely. Tristan's eyes were grey, and she looked deeply into them, studying each line and fold in the silver-blue irises. She had never seen eyes that color before, and they were a mystery to her. He did not look away.

The servant returned and cleared his throat, breaking their mutual gaze. He brought saké in a porcelain bottle with two matching cups and poured them each a drink.

"I am famished, Ambassador," Tristan said. "Will you join me in some supper? I understand that the kitchen has a most excellent stewed hen."

"Then how can I refuse?" She replied. Keiko probably should have declined, since it had been arranged for her to meet another guest for dinner, but she didn't want the handsome ambassador to go. She glanced at the doors again.

"Stewed hen for you both, then?" the servant asked.

"Yes, and bring rice and *unagi* as well," Keiko added.

"As you wish." The servant bowed and left.

"*Unagi*," Tristan said with a smile. "I am quite fond of eels." Then he raised the small cup of saké in his hand. "*Kanpai.*"

Keiko raised hers as well. "Cheers."

The saké was smooth and tasted expensive. She'd have expected nothing less at the Trade Summit – only the highest quality food and beverages from each delegate's own country would do. The ambassadors had brought their own chefs as well, to select their most impressive dishes and make sure the food was optimally prepared. As this was her first ambassadorial function, her chef was also a *bushi*, a *samurai*, who reported directly to her father, and was meant to protect her. And keep her in line.

Keiko smiled at Tristan and felt her cheeks getting warm. She blamed it on the saké.

"Is this your first visit to the island?" Tristan asked.

"It is."

"I have spent a great deal of time here – English winters can be cold and wet. Shall I give you a tour? As an ambassador, you will be visiting often, I suspect."

"Perhaps that is so," she said. "I accept your invitation. I will, of course, bring my chaperone."

"Indeed. I would insist upon it."

Keiko smiled shyly, as protocol demanded, and fidgeted with her braid. She was not as innocent as he seemed to think she was, but she stood to lose nothing by not correcting him.

"I wonder if your wife might like to come on the tour as well?"

He held her gaze and smiled. "Alas, I am not yet so blessed as to have a wife."

Keiko inclined her head, hiding her own smile.

The servant and his helper brought their food. Their conversation slowed. Keiko, too, was hungry. Wearing forty-five pounds' worth of silk robes all day was tiring, even for one as strong as her. As much as she was enjoying Ambassador Rathmore's attention, she would be glad to return to her quarters, where her lady-in-waiting would help her remove the twelve layers of kimonos, coat, and apron. Perhaps she would even take her exercise and get some air. But there was one more task to complete. She spared another glance at the doors.

Keiko set down her silver chopsticks. "I have had chicken prepared in many ways, but nothing like this. I insist that you provide my chef with the recipe."

"Only if you will instruct your chef to provide mine with his recipe for roasted eels."

Keiko smiled shyly and promptly got lost in Tristan's eyes again. A fantasy of him undressing her instead of her faithful lady-in-waiting flashed into her mind. Just as quickly, she dismissed it. That might happen at a later date, but this was neither the time nor place. Regrettably.

The double doors swung open, and Vladimir Alkamet swept through them. He was not unhandsome – thick black hair, ends burnished golden by the sun, fell just past his shoulders, framing his high, regal cheekbones. Hard muscles rippled under his tunic as he moved, and all the other diners turned to watch him pass. A long black cloak flared out behind him. Keiko followed him with her eyes, her face impassive.

Ignoring Tristan, he bowed to her when he reached the table. "Good evening, milady."

Keiko smiled demurely. Her father had arranged this dinner, so it behooved her to feign

Page ❤ 148

interest, even as she chaffed at her father's authority. The last thing she wanted to do right now was to negotiate a rice export contract.

"Good evening." She inclined her head slightly in deference to the new arrival.

Vladimir gave Tristan a hard look sat down in the chair across from Keiko. Tristan, however, looked amused.

"Ambassador Rathmore, might I introduce Mr. Vladimir Alkamet?"

"Alkamet and I are acquainted." He smiled politely.

Vladimir smirked. "It has been some time, Rathmore. I am delighted that you were able to join Keiko and me for our engagement dinner."

Keiko blinked rapidly a few times. "I beg your pardon. I believe you mean dinner engagement. It was my understanding that we were to discuss a business proposition to export rice to your country. Nothing more."

Tristan sat straighter in his chair.

"You are correct that there was a proposition – I made it to your father. Your hand in marriage was part of the agreement."

My father would not do this to me! Would he? Marriages as political alliances were very common, even with her kind. But the Alkamets were warriors and warlords, not kings. Not even nobility of any sort. She didn't understand why her father would choose to ally himself with them, and even less why he felt he would need to cement this alliance with a marriage.

Keiko's mind raced, trying to find a way to refute his claim. "I have had no message from my father. You understand that I require some proof of this alleged agreement."

Alkamet reached into the folds of his tunic and pulled out a roll of mulberry paper tied with a red ribbon and handed it to her.

Keiko read the document. Then she read it again. It was a contract for rice exported from Japan to Rus. And there was a clause stipulating the marriage between Keiko Ogoncho and Vladimir Alkamet. Her father's seal, a white dragon and a golden bird on a crimson background, was at the bottom of the paper. She studied the picture carefully.

Alkamet chortled. "I trust everything is in order?"

Tristan shifted in his chair. Keiko held the document up to the late afternoon sun. Then she smelled the seal.

When she set it down, her eyes glowed red with rage. "Fraud!" she shouted. "This is a forgery!" Her eyes narrowed to slits, and she quaked with fury. "How dare you?" she hissed.

Without warning, she shifted into the form of a small golden bird, her heavy *jūnihitoe* collapsing on the floor without her to hold it up. She flew up, high above the building, and let out a wail, then a shuddering screech. Then the tiny bird turned into a serpentine white dragon. Her scales were like pearls, glistening in the sun, and her eyes flashed jade green.

The *samurai* came running from the kitchen, hand on his sword hilt. The other dragons on the balcony paused their meals to watch the show. But Keiko hardly gave her protector a glance.

Lightning flashed from her eyes, and storm clouds came boiling into the sky. The wind picked up, knocking over goblets and tearing white linen tablecloths from vacant tables. Alkamet quickly shifted into his dragon form and met her in the air. His glossy black scales were edged in gold, but they looked dull under the angry clouds. Tristan and the *samurai* joined them – the samurai blue-green with a trailing beard, and Tristan green as bottle glass.

Keiko glared at Alkamet. "You forget who I am," she snarled. "Remember that I am famine's daughter – when my father takes the form of the golden bird, hunger plagues the land. My calamity is of a different kind. I do not bring a shortage of food, but of offspring. For one generation of man, the wives of your clan will struggle to conceive, and few of the dragonlets that result will survive."

Alkamet opened his jaws as if to rake her with fire, but the clouds opened up, dousing him with cold rain.

"Do not test me further," Keiko snapped.

The *samurai* swooped in between them, and Alkamet backed off. He lowered his head and growled, "The seal was stolen from your father. How did you know the document was false?"

Keiko's lips pulled back into a frightening smile. "My father only uses true dragon's blood – his own – to seal his contracts. You used the pigment vermilion, from ground cinnabar, and also called dragon's blood. Crushed cinnabar carries the faint scent of rotten eggs. The blood of my father does not."

Alkamet glared, as if he had more to say, then thought better of it. He turned and flapped away, his great wings heaving against the wind.

"I believe we still have a dessert course," Tristan said.

Keiko nodded. The wind let up, and the clouds lightened and started to drift away.

"*Samurai*," she said. "see to it that our clothes are delivered to my suite." She nodded to the pile of wet silk garments that she had been wearing earlier.

The *samurai* scowled.

"Why don't we have dessert in my quarters?" she asked.

Tristan eyed the sodden *jūnihitoe* and nodded.

Then both dragons took to the air, silhouetted against the fading evening sun, as they flew around each other, weaving and twining together in an ancient dance.

Auld Lang Syne

Ellen Leventhal

THE LIGHTS in the fitting room showed every drop of cellulite. Jana furrowed her brow which didn't help. The creases in her face became more evident, and she was reminded of rivers on a map. Each wrinkle joining another to form a confluence of creases. She wondered why she let Kelly talk her into this. She was happy with the way her life was. Well, maybe not happy, but content.

"I don't think the yellow is the best for you," said Jana's daughter, Kelly.

"I don't think anything is the best for me these days, honey."

"Here, try this blue dress."

Jana took the dress from Kelly and held it up. She did like the blue. Blue and purple were always her colors.

"I can remember when you were little, I always wore purple with huge shoulder pad inserts," said Jana holding up the blue dress.

"And you wanted to look like a football player, why?" asked Kelly.

Jana laughed. "It was the style. The bigger the shoulder pads the better. After all, your shoulders needed to match your giant hair."

"You didn't look like a linebacker when you first dated Dad, did you?"

"No, that lovely fashion wasn't popular until you and Scott were little. When I met your dad in the late sixties, bell bottoms, mini skirts, and tie-dye were all the rage," Jana said. She chuckled remembering the outfit she wore on her first date with Sam. A dress so short it would be a shirt on her now.

Jana looked at Kelly and wondered where the time went. *Weren't she and Sam just changing Kelly and Scott's diapers?* Sam was a wonderful father. She missed him. Or maybe she just missed the way things were. But she was fine. Life had taken on the rhythm of a new normal the last several years. Sam and Jana were more than civil. They were there for the kids and each other when needed. They may even still love each other, but were no longer *in* love. Her life was calm now. No roller coaster emotions, no surprises. She wasn't unhappy. She just *was*.

Jana tugged the blue dress over her head. Unfortunately, the dress wasn't cooperating. The more she tugged, the more the dress resisted. When she finally got it over her frame, she frowned. She always had a curvy body, but now the curves had morphed into unsightly bulges.

"Knock knock, are you doing ok in there?" A way too cheerful saleslady called to them from outside the door.

"I think I need a bigger size," sighed Jana.

"No prob!" chirped the twenty-year-old size zero. "It's a pretty dress. My grandma just bought the same one."

Jana's face fell. *I'm not old enough to be that girl's grandmother*. She pulled her jeans back on, grabbed Kelly's hand, and left.

"I don't know how you talked me into going shopping," Jana said to her daughter. "It's just a date."

"But a very special one. And I want you to look great," answered Kelly.

Jana knew that ship had passed. She hadn't looked *great* in years. She felt old, bedraggled, and a bit like the Pillsbury Dough Boy.

Jana and Kelly walked the perimeter of the mall and looked down at the skaters in the rink below.

"Really, the ice rink is the only thing I like about this mall. The noise, the stores, and the pushy salespeople give me a headache," Jana said.

She didn't like crowds, and the hustle and bustle of the mall made her jittery. However, Jana's desire to make her daughter happy outweighed her aversion to the Galleria. Anyway, this was a day for mother-daughter bonding, and she would do it anywhere. She loved seeing her daughter happy, and if a day of date prep would make her only daughter smile, then she would do it. After all, Kelly would be going back to Seattle after the first of the year, and Jana cherished every moment they had together.

Kelly took her mother's hand and led her towards another store. "Come on," she said. "It's not so bad, and we're going to find you the perfect dress for your perfect date."

"So if the date is going to be perfect, I assume the guy is too, correct?" Jana asked.

"Absolutely! Couldn't be more perfect," said Kelly.

"Can't you give me more information about this perfect guy you've found for me?" asked Jana.

"Just that he's about your age, and I think you'll have some things in common."

Jana loathed being set up, but she'd do it for her kids. Always for her kids. Especially ever since Sam left.

She plastered on a happy face, but the incessant Christmas music was getting on Jana's nerves. "Why are they still playing this music?" she asked Kelly. "It's almost New Year's."

"Don't be a Grinch. Anyway, we're here to get you all fixed up for your date. Today's not about anything but you," said Kelly.

"So if it's about me, give me some details about this Mr. Wonderful you and your brother found for me," Jana said.

"OK. He's the father of a good friend," Kelly told her mother. "And I know you'll like him. Now let's get going."

Jana was happily surprised when they reached the next store. The sales people were not overly young, overly pushy, or at all anorexic. Music wasn't blaring, and the dresses looked longer than tube tops. After trying a few, she settled on a purple A-line. It was a wool blend with a V-neck, just low enough to be interesting, but not low enough to show too much. "Nobody wants to see old lady cleavage," she told Kelly.

"You look beautiful, Mom," Kelly said smiling.

"Well, I don't look like I was stuffed into a sausage skin, so I'll take it," Jana replied.

"And Dad always liked you in purple," added Kelly. Jana shot her a look.

"It's not about Dad anymore, Kelly, and you know it," Jana said. "It's been a long time, honey," she added.

Kelly looked down at her shoes and ignored the comment. "Time for accessories," she said. "And your date really is Mr. Wonderful."

Jana hooked arms with her daughter and flashed her a smile of resignation. "Let's get this over with then," she said.

When they reached *Lulu's Accessories*, on the other side of the mall, the smell of Cinnabon and Mrs. Fields reminded Jana that she hadn't eaten yet. "What do you think?" she asked. "Just a small bite wouldn't hurt, right?"

Before Kelly could answer, they heard a loud crash, a pop, and some screams. Not knowing what is was, they scrambled into the store.

"There's a shooter," whispered an elderly lady decked out in an overabundance of bangle bracelets.

"I'll get him!" yelled a deranged looking man. "I'm a trained Ninja! Who's with me?"

Jana and Kelly looked at each other. Just in case, they crouched down behind a cut out of Rudolf; his red nose flicking on and off to the beat of the man's rants.

"I can work with the Ninja!" cried a frail-looking elderly woman. "I have a black belt in karate. I got it in 1955!"

"And I can fence!" added a pre-teen girl. She jumped out from behind a rack of scarves and thrust her orange umbrella at the crowd. "En garde!"

The store security guard sighed and hoisted himself off his chair. "Calm down, everyone," he said. "I'd have been told if there was a shooter. I'll find out what that noise was." He walked to a corner and said something into his walkie-talkie.

"If it's not a shooter, I'm sure it's a bomb," said a beautifully coifed Ralph Lauren-clad woman. She gazed down at her carefully manicured hands. "We will most likely die here, and it's Obama's fault!" A chorus of agreeing sentiments sailed through the air.

"They'd have told me if it was a bomb too," added the guard, shaking his head. "Hold on. I'm finding out what happened." His walkie-talkie crackled, and he picked it up. Jana couldn't hear what was being said, but she noticed the guard laughing.

"You can all go back to your shopping now, folks," he said. "Just a little mishap in the toy section."

"Well, that's a relief. Let's check out these earrings," said Kelly.

I don't need earrings, I need a Xanax, thought Jana, but she went along with her daughter's wishes.

Jana chose the least glitzy pair of earrings that she could find, paid at the front, and left the store. As the two made their way out of the mall, they noticed that the toy section looked like a small disaster area. Jana pointed out a contrite looking boy with his head down talking to a man in a suit. The boy was pulling at his sleeve and mumbling something about being sorry and not knowing that hover boards could actually go so fast. The gaping hole in the wall and the faint smell of smoke told the story.

When they got home, Kelly went upstairs to her old bedroom. The pink comforter and aqua walls in her room hadn't changed since she was a little girl. "How come you never changed this room? You know, into a gym or something?" she called to Jana.

Jana was across the hall in her room hanging up her new dress. "A gym? Do I look like I use a gym?" she asked with a laugh. "And anyway, I guess there's something comforting in seeing things as they used to be."

Kelly appeared at Jana's door. "It's time to look ahead, Mom, not backwards. So, do you want me to come with you to your hair appointment later?"

"Sure, why not?" Jana answered. "Especially since this whole makeover thing is your idea. Maybe we'll have another adventure. You never know when somebody will ride a flaming hover board through the wall."

"It wasn't flaming," Kelly said smiling. "It was just a little overheated."

When Kelly went downstairs, and Jana was alone, she opened her nightstand drawer. She dug under a pile of books and papers to retrieve a long hidden picture of Sam. "Your college girl is finally changing her looks, Sam. I wonder if you'd like it," she whispered.

"Lunchtime!" Kelly called, pulling Jana back to reality. "I cooked! Well, Kraft cooked, but I heated," she added.

The two enjoyed a late lunch and then drove to town. They parked a few blocks from the salon, determined to enjoy the unusually cool and sunny day. Jana loved her little town and enjoyed strolling the streets and looking into boutiques. Maybe the day would turn out ok.

When they reached the small Craftsman-style structure that housed the hair salon, they found that Jana's regular stylist, Carrie, was in Jamaica with her newest boyfriend. Jana's jaw dropped when she saw who would be taking Carrie's place. The intricate tattoos that cuffed the girl's arms were actually kind of interesting, but what was that in her nose?

"That's a nose ring, Mom, don't worry. She's fine," Kelly said.

"I'm not stupid, I know what nose rings are, but look at hers. Why is it reflecting the light like that?" Jana couldn't help staring.

"You're being rude, Mom!" Kelly chided her mother.

"And her hair...what color is that?" whispered Jana. She went to the front desk. "I think I'll wait until Carrie..."

A shrill voice broke in. "You must be Jana! I'm Aphrodite! Carrie told me you may be ready for a change. A big date coming up?"

"I guess," mumbled Jana.

Jana had dated a bit when Sam first left, but nothing ever came of it. There was the psychologist who analyzed her every word and movement, the car salesman who tried to sell her a bill of goods, and the accountant who looked too much like Sam for her comfort. After a while, she swore off men. Friends tried to set her up, but she wasn't interested. The only reason she agreed to this date is because of Kelly and Scott. Her compulsion to try and make her children happy.

"We're going to make you even more beautiful than you are now," said Aphrodite and led Jana to the large, granite shampoo bowl. "You look tense," she said.

"I'm ok, just a bit of a headache," Jana replied.

"Let me help you." Aphrodite waved light blue crystals over Jana's head. "Better now?" she asked. Without waiting for an answer, Aphrodite lowered the chair, placing Jana's head near the bowl. "Comfy honey?"

"Well, I think my head is back a little too far," said Jana.

"What honey?" Aphrodite asked massaging Jana's head and neck.

Jana gave in and closed her eyes. Soon the whole salon was spinning. Water and shampoo dripped into her eyes, but when she tried to sit up to protest, dizziness overcame her, and she fell backward hitting her head on the shampoo bowl.

"Oh Vishnu!" cried Aphrodite, "Are you ok?"

"I think so," Jana said. "I forgot to mention that I have a bit of vertigo. I can't lean my head back too far."

" I can totally cleanse your aura, and the vertigo will never return," said Aphrodite, holding Jana's head in her hands. Her fingers danced on Jana's face.

"No, no, please. Just help me sit up. My aura is fine," said Jana.

"Ok, honey. This is it. You are going to love the new you."

Aphrodite fluttered around with some kind of potion. "We need to lighten this up. And oh, those eyebrows! We'll do something about that too."

As Aphrodite chattered about new looks and cleansed auras, Jana felt a sharp pain in her eye. Her hand instinctively flew up to cover it, but that only made the pain worse. "I'm not sure what's happening, but can you help me?" she asked.

"Sure, honey."

"But please don't ...."

It was too late. With a whirl of the chair, Jana's world turned upside down again. Not only was her eye stinging, but she felt like she was falling head first into a dark hole. And then the voices.

"What's wrong?"

"Just breathe deeply. Your chakras are out of balance."

"Why did you spin her?"

"Look at that bump on her head!"

"Mom! Your eye!" She recognized Kelly's voice even though she couldn't see her.

Aside from the bump on her head, her left eye was swollen shut. And then her head began to itch.

At that moment, Randall, the salon owner came rushing in. "Glory! What happened to you, girl?"

Jana moaned and Kelly introduced herself. She explained the situation. "Well, that won't do. We will fix this right now!" He sent Aphrodite to the back to get a clean cloth to put on Jana's eye. And ice for her head. "What shampoo did you use on this poor girl?" Randall called.

Deep sobs. "The regular stuff. I'm so sorry." Aphrodite came back with the cloth. "I'm so sorry, Jana."

"Don't worry about it. It's not your fault. You were trying your best," Jana said, scratching her head. *I should NOT be going on this date.*

Randall continued working on Jana. "She tries a little too hard," he said. "It's the whole *Aphrodite* thing. Talking about chakras and all that."

"What do you mean?"

"Well," whispered Randall looking around. "Between you and me, her real name is Gertrude. She wants to impress people. She's a sweet kid, though."

Randall told Jana to relax and assured her that blonde highlights would make her look and feel like a new woman. An hour later, it did. A swollen eyed, bumpy headed, itchy, exceptionally blond woman.

"Oh Mom," said Kelly hugging her mother. "I didn't know you were so allergic to ... well everything. But you look beautiful, anyway."

Jana was too busy scratching her scalp to listen. "It's too blonde. I look like Harpo Marx."

"Who?" asked Kelly.

"Never mind. Can we please just go home now?" By the time they left the salon, the weather had changed. They stepped outside to see ominous clouds hovering above. *Now, what?* thought Jana. And the skies opened.

When they got to the car, Jana's new hairdo was ruined, and her clothes were sticking to her. Rain pelted the windows as they drove, making it difficult to see. "Good thing I'm driving," Kelly said trying to lighten the atmosphere.

Jana gave her a sharp look with her one working eye.

"The universe is telling me something. I should NOT be going on this date," said Jana. They sat in silence the rest of the way home. *I'm too old for this.*

When they got home, the rain had subsided, and they decided to relax out on the patio and enjoy some Margaritas. Sitting there watching the sun go down behind the palms made life seem almost normal. Except that Jana had a splitting headache, a swollen eye, and hair that made her look like a slutty Golden Retriever.

"Dad would like this. You know, the view," said Kelly.

"Yes, he did love it here. There's something inherently soothing about this place."

"There are other things Dad liked, Mom. Don't forget that." Kelly grinned at her mother. Jana threw a towel at her and drained her Margarita glass.

Kelly's phone rang. "Sure," she said into the phone. "I think that will be fine. See you then."

"Hot date?" Jana asked.

"Not quite, but I do need to go. You'll be ok, right?"

"Sure. Go. Have fun. I need to plan my lectures for next semester, anyway."

The wind picked up, and the fronds on the palm tree swayed. Jana used to love the dancing shadows the fronds made. Now she worried about them falling on someone's head. She didn't know exactly when things changed. Little things that once made her smile now made her anxious.

She couldn't focus on her work, so she trudged up the stairs, exhausted and a bit drunk. Crawling into bed, she was acutely aware that she was alone. She and Sam had not been together for years, but every once in a while, the aloneness crept up on her like a thief in the night.

When Jana drifted off to sleep, she dreamed of life the way it was. She dreamed about tie-dyed shirts, Sam's VW bus, and rocking babies to sleep. She awoke in the morning feeling like she was in a fog. She remembered the margaritas. Then she remembered her eye. She dragged herself out of bed and into the bathroom. *I look like crap*, she thought. Her head was pounding, but whether it was due to last night's margaritas or the bump on her head, she didn't know.

Hearing the T.V downstairs, Jana smiled. Kelly was home. She made her way down the stairs, and Kelly waved.

"Tonight's the night," Kelly said with a smile that could rival the Cheshire Cat's.

The date. She didn't want to go, but she would, even though she thought it was silly. Going on a blind date was never a good idea, but it was totally ridiculous on New Year's Eve. She wondered what Sam was doing this year. She tried to remember how many New Year's Eves they had spent together, but she couldn't recall.

"How's the bump?" Kelly asked.

"Not bad," answered Jana. "But look at my eye." It was still swollen, but at least, it was open. How did I ever let you talk me into this? And New Year's Eve, yet?" New Year's Eve, once a fun night full of promise for the future, had become a reminder of things lost.

"Yesterday was crazy, I know," Kelly said, "but you'll have a great time tonight. Just don't go to the mall or get your hair done, and you'll be fine," she said winking. "I know this guy's son pretty well, and he swears his dad is even nicer than he is. And he's a pretty great guy."

Sipping her coffee and nursing her head, Jana asked, "How will I know him?"

"He'll know you. I told him about your purple dress. And don't worry about it being New Year's Eve."

"Shoot me now," muttered Jana. She gulped her coffee.

After a few leisurely hours of reading and relaxing (and tending to her eye) it was time to get ready for the date. Jana willed herself to get off the couch and went upstairs to begin the great transformation. After she squeezed herself into her Spanx, fixed her hair the best she could, and put a gallon of make-up on her eye, she decided that she wasn't the horror she thought she was. She would never admit it out loud, but she was a bit intrigued about Kelly and Scott's Mr. Wonderful. *Maybe this will be ok.*

Jana and her date were planning to meet at the Top of the Mark. It was a popular restaurant and sure to be crowded. She'd seen enough crime shows to know not to meet a stranger in a secluded place or have him pick her up at her house. Not wanting to drive on New Year's Eve, she called a cab.

Kelly was on her way out for the evening. As she left, she called, "Have fun, Mom. Give this guy a chance. Happy New Year!"

Jana had just finished putting on her lipstick when the cab blew its horn. *This is it*, she thought. She grabbed a long sweater, jumped into her way too high heels, and headed out the door. "Happy New Year, ma'am. I'm John. At your service. Where are we going tonight?" asked the cabbie.

"To the Top of the Mark restaurant, please. Do you know where that is?"

"Of course! Pretty snazzy. You must have a hot date," said the cabbie.

Seriously? thought Jana. "Just a date. How hot is still to be determined."

The driver zigzagged through the crowded streets at a pace that made Jana nervous. She leaned over the seat. "I'm not in a hurry!" The cabbie couldn't hear her over the radio and the street noise. And the fact that he was on the phone.

"Please hang your phone up!" Jana called. "This sign back here says you will not be on the phone. It's dangerous!"

Page ❤ 172

"Can't hear you, ma'am! I'm talking to my brother in New York. I need to talk to my niece before she goes to sleep."

"But can't you call her later?"

The cabbie continued his call. "Sure Princess, I'll sing you a song. *Twinkle, twinkle...*"

Jana slumped down in her seat and closed her eyes trying to focus on something other than the cabbie and his singing. She knew she shouldn't be going on this date. All the signs have been pointing to it. She almost got shot at the mall (ok, that was a false alarm, but still it was scary), she had an allergic reaction to everything at the salon, and now this.

"Here we are!" said John. Jana opened her eyes and took a deep breath. She was in front of the restaurant. She smoothed her dress and began to get out of the car. As she lifted her leg, she felt something sticky. Great. Chewing gum. The back of her dress had chewed bubble gum all over it. She got out and tried to get it off. John jumped out of his cab and began to help her. He bent down to peel the gum off her rump in front of one of the fanciest restaurants in town.

"Well hello, Jana!" she heard someone call. "Are you ok? Is that man bothering you?"

"No, it's fine, Father Murphy, I'm fine, thanks. Happy New Year." She felt her face redden.

"OK, then. Happy New Year to you," said Father Murphy. "Hope to see you at church soon."

Jana grinned uncomfortably and waved.

John was still working on her backside. "I've almost got it, Miss!" he said.

"That's fine!" Jana snapped. "Please go. Oh, and happy New Year." She handed him a wad of bills. "Thank you."

Then she was alone. Puffy eye, bumpy head, Harpo Marx hair, and sticky rear end; standing outside the Top of the Mark. She wondered if the date could get any worse once it actually started. She walked inside and sat down at the bar. She tried to relax, but something was gnawing at her. This wasn't the night to go on a date. Forty- five years earlier, she and Sam had exchanged vows. They had a small wedding, just their family and close friends. Jana and Sam both wanted to get married on the beach. They planned to wait until the summer and pledge their love with the water lapping at their toes, and the sounds of The Beach Boys swirling around them. But things happen. And a baby is what happened to them. They got married sooner than they planned, but they never looked back. At least not for many years. *We were so young*, she thought. It wasn't easy raising two kids so young, but she and Sam felt like they owned the world. She often wondered how that feeling slipped away. She missed Sam, but she wasn't really sure why. Oh well, no time for that now. Time to look sharp and get ready for Mr. Wonderful.

"I'm Roy. Happy New Year. What can I get you?" asked the bartender.

"I'd like a Pinot Grigio, please."

"Sure thing. I can put that on your tab. What name is your reservation under?" She realized that she had no idea of the last name of her date.

"Um, Blake, I think." *Was Blake his first name or last? What did Kelly say?* "That's not necessary, I'll just pay now with cash," Jana said.

She took the chilled glass and handed Roy a ten. The bar was crowded with players. It made her feel old. She thanked the bartender for the drink, told him to keep the change, and pulled her gummy dress off the cushion of the bar stool. Knowing she had a big splotch on her rear end, she yanked on her sweater and checked that it was all the way down. Jana hopped off the stool and toddled in her too high heels over to a small table near a window. She took a few sips of her wine and it went immediately to her head. She realized that she hadn't eaten much all day. A waitress walked around with appetizers, and Jana grabbed a few. Within fifteen minutes, her stomach cramped, and her hands began to shake. "Is there shrimp in these?" she asked the waitress.

"Yes, do you like it?"

"Yes I do, but it doesn't like me," answered Jana. *Why didn't she ask what it was first?* Her stomach reeled. *What else can go wrong?* she thought. She didn't have to wait long for an answer.

"Hi, doll." *Am I in a bad fifties musical?* A man sat down at her table, pulled the chair in, and clinked her glass. "To the new year, beautiful." Jana could smell the booze on his breath. She knew it wasn't smart, but she continued to drink her wine. She was feeling a bit nauseous and more than a bit tipsy. She had no idea who this person was, and she didn't want to find out. *Was this her date?* "Let me get you a fresh drink," he said. "Then we can get to know each other better. I had no idea my date would be so foxy! Those kids have good taste!" His hand began to travel up her leg. *Foxy? Is this the seventies? Those kids? Oh, God, this IS my date.*

"Excuse me," she said, pulling away. "I'm going to the restroom."

"Don't forget to come back, doll," he said chuckling.

She gave him a thumbs up. "You got it, sweet cheeks."

There was no way she was going to go back to that table. He was disgusting and sleazy, and anyway, she was getting sicker by the minute. Needing to escape, she maneuvered her way through the crowd. She began to shiver. She pulled her sweater tight around her body, but it didn't help. Her stomach roiled, and she knew she wouldn't last long. She got to the restroom and pressed against the door. It wouldn't open. Pushing harder, it gave way, and she found herself face down on the floor. She pulled herself up to her knees and crawled to a stall where she emptied the contents of her stomach.

Sweat poured down her face. Her pulse was racing. She had to get out. Fumbling in her purse, she found her phone and hit speed dial.

"Hey, you've reached Kelly. Leave a message!"

"Honey, I'm sick. I'm grabbing a cab and going home. Please let what's his name know."

How could they have set me up with this guy? This is NOT Mr. Wonderful.

She felt like she had been hit by a truck. Her head was pounding, and the wine wasn't helping.

A knock on the door. "Hey doll, you ok in there?"

Could there be a worse date? "I'm not feeling well. I just need a little time," she answered. Holding onto the wall, she raised herself up into a standing position.

"OK doll, I'll be at the bar."

She knew she was not going back to Mr. Sleaze. It may not be polite, but she was sick. It was more than a few shrimps and some wine. She was really sick. And even sicker of him. She tried calling the cab company, but couldn't get through. *What is that other place the kids talk about? Youber? Boober?* She didn't care how she looked. Her makeup was running, she had gum on her dress, and her breath could kill a young cow. But she had to leave the restroom at some point. She stumbled to a new table and thought about what to do. She felt utterly alone in a sea of people.

"Hey, doll!" Mr. Sleaze found her. *Can this really be happening?* He strode over to her and draped his sweaty arm around her shoulders. She pulled away. Thankfully his phone rang.

"Just a minute doll. Have another drink while I get this." He shoved a Jack and Coke in her face and picked up his phone.

What were my kids thinking? she wondered.

"What are you talking about?" Mr. Sleaze growled into the phone. "I'm with her now!" He turned to Jana. "So doll, you ain't Bambi?"

"Do I look like a Bambi? I'm a college professor, not a stripper."

"No need to get nasty," a female voice said. Jana looked around to see a long legs and a plunging neckline. "I'm Bambi, and this here guy is supposed to be my date. Oh, and I ain't a stripper. I'm an exotic dancer!" She threw a drink at Jana, and walked off with Mr. Sleaze.

At least he's gone, Jana thought. She wiped herself off and put her head down on the marble table. *This is the worse date ever, and my real date hasn't even shown up.* She was a bit insulted about being stood up, but she was too sick to worry about that. She just wanted to go home. But how?

Jana's head was still down on the table when she heard footsteps approach. *Now what?* "Are you ill?" a male voice asked. Eyes closed, head down, she sighed. *It can't be. Can it? The cologne, the voice. That feeling.*

"I think I'm your date," the man said. "You're wearing a purple dress, and that's what I was told you'd be wearing."

Jana didn't need to look up to know he'd be smiling. She knew his eyes would be crinkling up, and she knew he would soon break into laughter. A laugh that would touch her soul. She didn't move, but her heart beat faster. *Those kids*, she thought. She should have known. There were hints, but she was too thick to realize. *He's the father of a good friend. You'll have a lot in common.* She mumbled, "I have to leave. I'm sick."

"Well, maybe I can take you home."

Jana lifted her head and locked eyes with the man. "Are you sure I'm your date? I've been mistaken for someone's date once already tonight."

That laugh. "Nope. I was told my date would be in a purple dress. Look around. Nobody else in purple." His voice was soothing. He touched her cheek. It felt good. Not at all like Mr. Sleaze's grabby hands. "I asked a few people if they'd seen a lone woman in a purple dress. The hostess told me about some crazy lady wearing purple, pushing people to get to the restroom. I figured I should leave."

"What made you stay?" she asked.

"The bartender told me that she was kind of tipsy after a few sips of wine. Purple dress, drunk on wine. I thought I may want to get to know who that crazy lady is."

"Well, you do now. Still want to stay?"

"More than ever."

"I'm going to kill those kids of yours, Sam," Jana said.

"I'll help you," he replied.

"Kelly said your name was Blake. I should have figured it out. William Blake is the only poet you know," Jana told Sam.

"Tiger, Tiger burning bright," said Sam. A smile spread across his face. And his eyes did crinkle. "Scott said your name was Lily. If I had been thinking, I would have guessed."

"My favorite flower," Jana said.

"What do you want to do now?" Sam asked.

"Well, I'm sick. Can you take me home?"

"My pleasure," he said. Sam helped Jana get up and guided her to his car. "I've missed you. What happened to your eye?"

"I've missed you too," Jana said. "And my eye, well that's a long story."

"You're blonde," he said. "I like it. Let's get you home. We can talk then. After all, we *are* on a date. We should take the time to get to know each other."

"But, Sam, it's been years…"

"Let's think of this as the first date of the new year…a new start," he said.

They rode in silence to the house that they bought together and where they raised their kids. The house that was once their home. Jana wondered if they could bring back some of what they had.

Jana leaned on Sam as he helped her to the couch. He brought her tea and a warm blanket.

"Not very exciting for a first date," Sam said as Jana sipped the tea.

"A date, huh?" she murmured. She was trying to keep awake.

"Yes, I told you. Our first date. Again."

"Worst. First. Date. Ever," Jana said.

"Happy Anniversary, sweetie," added Sam.

Jana smiled and curled up under a blanket. "You too," she said before drifting off to sleep.

If you enjoyed this book,
please consider leaving a review
at your favorite book sharing site.

Visit our Facebook page
(https://www.facebook.com/SpaceCityScribes)
and
Sign up for our mailing list
so you can be the first to know about
new releases from
the Space City Scribes!

About the Editor

Monica Shaughnessy has a flair for creating characters and plots larger than her home state of Texas. Most notably, she's the author of the Cattarina Mysteries, a cozy mystery series starring Edgar Allan Poe's real-life cat companion. Ms. Shaughnessy has eleven books in print, including two young adult suspense novels, a middle grade superhero novel, an Easter picture book, a cozy mystery series, and numerous short stories. Customers have praised her work time and again, calling it "unique and creative," "fresh and original," and "very well written." If you're looking for something outside the mainstream, you'll find it in her prose. When she's not slaying adverbs and tightening plots, she's helping clients hone their own manuscripts. The best way to learn about her books is to join her mailing list, which can be found on her website: monicashaughnessy.com.

Mandy Broughton and Monica Shaughnessy are the writing duo behind author

Annie Basset and a soon-to-be-released cozy mystery series set in Texas. In book one, Ruby Nash and her cadaver-sniffing dog, Sasha, are hot on the trail of a missing person—her future stepfather—and leave no bone unturned. *Dead & Buried: No Bones* releases early 2016.

Other Books by Monica Shaughnessy:

Cattarina Mysteries*: The Tell-Tail Heart, The Black Cats, The Raven of Liberty, To the River, Mr. Eakins' Book of Cats*

Adult Thriller/Horror: *Lethal Lore, Season of Lies*

YA/Children's: *Universal Forces, Doom & Gloom, The Easter Hound*

Short Stories/Anthologies: *The Trash Collector, Space City 6*

About the Authors

Mandy Broughton loves books. She can always be found with a book in her hand and two more in a bag. She gravitates towards mysteries but enjoys science fiction and a good historical novel as well. In libraries and bookstores, Mandy tries to stay in areas appropriate for her age. This is not always possible as she tends to find herself with more middle grade and young adult novels upon leaving.

She has a trio of middle-grade mysteries—a missing hamster, a UFO, and some absent-minded grandparents—have all found their way into her novels. She also has an adult cozy, *The Cat's Last Meow*, and several short stories published in various anthologies. And you can always find free short stories at popular ebook retailers.

Mandy Broughton and Monica Shaughnessy are the writing duo behind author Annie Basset and a soon-to-be-released cozy mystery series set in Texas. In book one, Ruby Nash and her cadaver-sniffing dog, Sasha, are hot on the trail of a missing person—her future stepfather—and leave no bone unturned. *Dead & Buried: No Bones* releases early 2016.

For the record, while it is true she has spent more money on books than groceries, it only happened once. And due to the great invention of peanut butter sandwiches, her husband did not starve that month.

Visit her online at MandyBroughton.com or on twitter @MandyBroughton. She will talk to anyone who will listen in 140 characters or less.

Other Books by Mandy Broughton:

Cream Cape and the Case of the Missing Hamster: #1 (always free, ages 7+)

The Case of the Flying Saucer: #2 (ages 7+)

The Case of the Blue-Hair Heist: #3 (ages 7+)

The Color of Silence (always free, sci-fi, YA to adult)

The Cat's Last Meow (adult murder mystery)

Artemis Greenleaf

Artemis Greenleaf has always been fascinated by the mysterious, and she devoured fairy tales, folk tales and ghost stories since before she could read. In 1995, she had a near-death experience which turned her perception of the world upside down. She lived to tell the tale (and often does, in one form or another). Artemis lives in the suburban wilds of Houston, Texas with her husband, two children and assorted pets. She writes novels, short stories, and non-fiction, and her work has appeared in magazines. For more information, please visit artemisgreenleaf.com or follow her on Facebook and Pinterest.

Other Books by Artemis Greenleaf:

Adults: *The Hanged Man's Wife* ◘*The Magician's Children* ◘ *Color Me Blackthorne* Tweens and Teens: *Earthbound* ◘ *Cheval Bayard* ◘ *Confessions of a Troll* ◘ *Exit Point* Younger Readers *Brain's Vacation* ◘ *Carl the Vegetarian Vampire* As

Coda Sterling *Dragon by Knight* ◘ *Dragon Killer* Anthologies *Space City 6* ◘ *Tides of Impossibility* ◘ *First Last Forever*

Ellen Leventhal loves words. She loves reading them, writing them, and teaching them. Ellen began her teaching career as a special education teacher and continued as a classroom teacher, working with both elementary and middle school aged children. She knew she hit the jackpot when she realized that she had the ability to combine her two passions, teaching and writing. Each summer she teaches creative writing in the WITS/ Rice School Literacy and Culture Program's Creative Writing Camp. Although very happy teaching, Ellen's writer's dream came true when her first children's book, written with Ellen Rothberg, was published in 2006. The book, *Don't Eat the Bluebonnets*, was the beginning of the South Pasture Series. *Hayfest, A Holiday Quest* and *Bully in the Barnyard* soon followed. These books can be found on her website, E2books.com. Ellen's short stories can be found in *Space City 6* and *Kissed By An Angel*, an anthology of middle grade stories with all proceeds going to the Sturge-Weber Foundation.

Currently, Ellen is busy working on a middle grade chapter book, several other picture books, and a compilation of children's poetry. You can find out more about Ellen by following her blog at ellenleventhal.com.

Kaleigh Castle Maguire is a wife
and mother of three who loves fiction writing and reading fiction of all genres. She has a particular passion for young adult and children's books. Her debut YA science fiction novel, *Inside the Palisade* was released by Lodestone Books in August 2015. She is a member of RWA , AWP and SCBWI . She loves to blog about books, writing, and to interview authors when she can get them to agree (which they happily do most of the time). In July of 2014, she joined the blogging team at Luna Station Quarterly, a magazine devoted to female authors of speculative fiction. Kaleigh's flash fiction has appeared in publications including Writers Type, Delta Women, Tough Lit, Black Petals Magazine, Six Minute Magazine, Midlife Collage, Everyday Fiction, and Luna Station Quarterly. She has three e-novellas published by Books To Go Now: *Destiny*, *Dear John*, and *Ivory Tower*. In 2014, she came second in YA/MG/children's category in the Houston

Writers' Guild fiction contest for her draft fantasy manuscript, *Halfling*, and in 2014 she came third in the Writers Type Short Story contest for "In For A Penny," appearing in *Space City 6*, the Space City Scribes' first anthology. She has completed the fiction writing certificate programs at UCLA and Stanford, and is currently a student in the MFA program in Writing for Children and Young Adults at Vermont College of Fine Arts. You can follow Kaleigh on her blog (kcmaguire.com), via Twitter (@KaleighM) or on Facebook (facebook.com/kcmaguireauthor).

Other Books by K.C. Maguire:

Inside the Palisade
Destiny
Dear John
Ivory Tower